FLORIDIAN MAYHEM

AN ARCHIE AND ELISE MYSTERY

GRANT FIELDGROVE

Floridian Madness

By Grant Fieldgrove

Copyright 2021

Watch the Sky Media & Publishing

All rights reserved

ISB 978-0-578-87973-4

Published by Watch the Sky Media – Publishing Division

First edition: 2021

You could slit my throat and with my one last
gasping breath I'd apologize for bleeding on your shirt.

-Taking Back Sunday

ELiSE

Oh my gosh, we're finally here.

Our new home.

The boxes are unpacked, the furniture is set up in a semi-okay fashion, and the last moving truck is beep-beep-beeping its way down our driveway and out of my life forever.

We're a year late, but it feels like a hundred. We were all set to move last June but, well, the country turned into a disease-ridden hellscape and all our plans changed – our house that was being built was put on hold. We were forced to spend over a year with zero entertainment in the middle of Montana, a state with not much entertainment to begin with.

But whatever, we made it. We're officially Floridians.

The weather here is quite the contrast to what I'm used to, and I absolutely love it. The sun is glowing, the air is hot and sticky sweet, I'm wearing the shortest shorts I can get away with without making my kids scream in disgust and a bikini top is doubling as my bra.

It's glorious.

Goodbye wretched snow. I hope I never see you again.

It's so lovely out here that I almost don't even want to go inside. Maybe I'll just stay out in the driveway for a little longer and soak up the rays.

"*Gawd, Mom*, can those shorts get any shorter?"

Well, so much for that. Eric, my oldest, is now standing by my side, giving me a look that he uses quite often now and that, honestly, I'm not too fond of.

He's had a rough year, just as all of us have, but his started right at the most challenging time for a growing boy, if you know what I mean. He shot up about a foot and in no time he'll be as tall as me...and then taller. Terrifying.

"Mind your own beeswax," I tell him, then give him a behind-the-back kick in the butt. He smiles.

"I'm glad we made it."

I wrap my arm around his shoulders and pull him close. I'm sure he's cringing internally but at least he is kind enough to not show it. "Kid," I say, "so am I."

It's so quiet out here that I can hear the waves crashing below. This is pure perfection.

If you're wondering how we ended up here, I'll tell you.

A year and a half ago, my husband and I were on a case where we got trapped in a mansion during a fierce snowstorm. As ridiculous as this sounds, the other guests began getting picked off one at a time by a mysterious, cloaked figure, which sort of, ya know, killed the mood, to say the least.

Somehow, we survived the night and walked away from it with more money than I ever dreamed of having, all thanks to an insanely generous paycheck from our deceased client that was paying us to be there.

Long story short, we made enough money to move us, my best friend Jamie, and two other families we adore, to the eastern coast of Florida, just south of Cocoa Beach and Cape Canaveral, and north of Palm Beach – a small little town called Sunrise Cove.

Now, just like some weird fairytale, we all live on the same street, four houses in a row, in a newly finished neighborhood called Bodfish Bay.

Don't ask me what a Bodfish is.

Anyway, we're here now, and I plan on packing in as much fun as humanly possible, for at least the first month or so. You never realize all the things you take for granted until literally everything comes to a halt and you're left in your house with a very stir-crazy family and absolutely nothing to do except go for drives and play board games.

I don't need to tell you. I'm sure you and everyone else shared our pain.

One good thing about having all that time on my hands was that I was able to accomplish something that has been a dream of mine since I was a little girl in dance class, before everything went wrong, before I became a teenage runaway, back when I still believed anything was possible for me.

I founded my own community theater.

After doing a little research about the area we were moving to, I noticed there wasn't a single place for live theater, so, well, I made my own.

Owning my own community theater wasn't actually the dream of that skinny little bright-eyed girl of my past, but it's close enough. I dreamed of being on the stage, but nowadays, being behind it is just as good.

It's not open yet, but now that everything is getting back to normal, it shouldn't take too long now. I hope that it will draw people from all along the coast, not just our small town.

More on that later, but I just wanted to catch you up on something I am very proud of.

"They're back," Eric says, my arm still around him, which is some sort of record.

"Oh dear."

My husband Archie is pulling our friend's truck into the driveway. Loaded in the bed is a box so big it's literally hanging over the edge, ready to fall out with any sudden movement. He made the turn so slowly it was like he was riding on four blown tires.

Eric is laughing. "It doesn't even fit in the truck! This is awesome!"

I sigh, trying not to laugh. Archie wanted to buy the biggest TV they make at the beginning of quarantine, but I convinced him to just wait until we got to Florida. At the time, I didn't know how long this whole thing would last, and now judging by the size of the box dangling out the back of Tabitha's ex-husband's truck, I feel like I made the right decision.

"This is gonna be so sweet, Mom!" Eric yelps, pulling away from me and bouncing towards the truck.

Archie puts the truck in park and steps out, the smile on his face so wide it looks like he has extra teeth. He looks at me like a kid on Christmas morning and says, "Duuuuuuuuude!"

"How big is that?" I say, getting a good look at the box this monstrosity is packaged in. "We measured the wall... remember?"

"Yeah," he says, "I... Of course, I remember. It's the one we... ya know, it's the one we agreed on. Remember, it's the one that... Ya know... We measured and said, Yeah, that one... that one will..."

He's stuttering.

Archie can lie his way through anything with anybody... except me. This is proof.

"It'll fit!" he says, way too loudly. "I mean, unless your measurements were wrong." He tries to laugh but his throat is as dry as sawdust. The laugh turns into a cough and I know that there is no way this will fit.

"Come on, babe, it's a statement piece!"

"A statement to whom, exactly?"

Archie thinks about this for a moment. He clearly wasn't expecting a follow-up question to his totally asinine remark.

"To us!" he says triumphantly. "I mean, come on, did you ever think you'd have a TV this big?"

I take a deep breath and just go with it. Sure. Fine. Whatever.

As long as it makes him happy then I'm fine with it.

It's not going to fit, though.

ARCHiE

Okay, so maybe Elise is slightly annoyed with me because we measured the wall the TV was going on... twice. According to our calculations, it was supposed to fit perfectly on this stained-oak stand we just had delivered and everything was going to work out great.

For a brand new 82-inch 4K TV.

The problem, and the source of Elise's mild annoyance, is that when I got to the store, I saw that they had a new TV that was four inches bigger.

Eighty-six inches!

So, naturally, I got that one.

Unbeknownst to me at the time, its feet are two inches too wide to fit on the new stand and, well, the screen is almost four inches too big for the wall. So, for now, it will have to sit on the floor and hang out past the corner and into the hallway a little bit. And, the expensive oak thing that Elise picked out is pretty much useless now. It's too big for any other room and too small for this, so, yeah.

Maybe I messed up, but it's not the end of the world. I even tried to play it off like *our* measurements were wrong and it was an honest mistake. Ya know, sharing the blame to save her feelings.

It took Elise about three seconds to see through that lie and point out the huge, and clearly visible, 86" in the left corner of the box.

I shrugged and said *oopsie*, which was met with an eye roll and defeated sigh.

"It's literally hanging out into the hallway."

"Yes," I say, unable to think of anything more clever.

"We're going to bang our shins on it every time we walk into the room."

"Also, yes."

"The dogs are going to hit it and knock it over."

"Possibly, also, yes."

Elise just laughs and leaves the room.

Whatever! We made it! We're here. In our new home. Finally!

What a strange and awful year and a half.

Our non-verbal and clearly autistic three-year-old, Gary, missed out on a crucial year of early-intervention because of this stupid virus that shut the country down. We had to do all we could, flying blind, trying to help him in any way possible. We used the YouTube teaching method, as in, we had no idea what to do, so we You-Tubed it. It was as awful as anticipated.

But, now that we're here, our top priority is getting him a (late) early-intervention so we can get him as much help as possible. Fortunately, during our quarantine, we were able to find all the right places to contact and we can get started on this in a week or two. We're just waiting on a call.

In the meantime, he's a happy kid and content with whatever we offer him, despite being heavily delayed in every childhood milestone possible, aside from breaking all my stuff.

The other kids and their friends couldn't be happier to be here. Eric and Elliot are thrilled to be able to wear shorts and t-shirts again, as am I, which was my standard professional daily outfit before thinking it would be a good idea to move to Montana... seriously... MONTANA!

It's like we stepped out of a freezer and into an oven. A wonderful, fantastic, oven. The air is actually wet here. Not that horrible Montana wet where it's just cold and disgusting – this is like the air is sweating on you. Florida humidity is like a big fat dude giving you a bear hug. There is nothing cold about this place and, at least for now, I love it. If I ever see snow again, it'll be too soon. I love it here so much that I may even go down to the beach from time to time. Who knows, maybe the Atlantic Toilet will be a little better than the Pacific

Toilet, which was always ice cold, and the sand fostered these horrible little sand-flies that were just awful.

But, for now, the TV is set up, as ridiculous as it looks, and all I want to do is open the windows, turn the AC on, and watch a crappy movie. Nobody knows I'm here so there should be no random calls from strangers begging for our help, ruining our days with their terrible problems they want us to solve.

In Florida, neither Elise nor I am licensed as a private investigator, however, I suspect that won't last long for Elise. I'm hoping her theater draws her full attention, and she can spend her time doing that instead of risking her life to help others, but who knows. She's much more ambitious than I am, so anything is possible.

I grab the remote, my giant screen flickers to life, and I'm about to make a movie selection when my phone rings.

Ugh.

I reach into my pocket and answer the call, despite my desire to smash it against the wall. But, whatever, it's not like the old days. The odds of this call being about a case are slim to none, so what's the harm?

"Yello?" I say, fully expecting to be asked about my car's extended warranty.

"Is this Archie Lemons?"

"Sure is. Can I still get that warranty if my car is currently on fire?!"

"Excuse me?"

Oops. "Oh... sorry. Hi, yeah, this is Archie Lemons..."

"My name is Sarah Benson... I saw your movie and heard you moved down here."

God damn it.

A few years back, Elise and I were the subjects of a reasonably successful comedy-mystery type flick starring Rachel McAdams as Elise and Jonah Hill as yours truly, despite the fact we look literally nothing alike.

On top of that, the movie depicted me as a bumbling idiot. I can't remember ever once falling down in real life, but good lord, Movie Archie took more pratfalls than Jack Tripper.

At one point, Movie Me was shirtless and fell through a glass patio table. Hilarity ensued.

The movie is a couple years old now and from what I thought, and hoped, entirely off the radar of most people, especially after the prospects of a sequel went down the tubes due to studio infighting.

Just fine with me. I can't imagine how far my stupidity would have been cranked up for a sequel.

"You remember the movie?" I ask, trying to hide the annoyance in my voice and wishing that it really *was* a scam call. I hope this call isn't what I think it is, but...

"Oh yeah, of course, it was... Well, I guess other parts of the country, they took this virus thing more seriously than here and closed all the movie theaters so no new releases came out, but our theaters were still open but we didn't have anything to see, and your movie was one of the ones that showed quite often."

The pandemic screws me again.

"Everyone knows who you are now down here, ya know, especially since the news hit that you guys were moving here. I mean, we tried to focus more on positive news and not all those people dying, you know?"

Oh god, take a breath, girl.

Sigh.

Maybe we should have moved to Miami instead of a small beach town. There is no way this would have made the news in any city with a population of over fifteen thousand.

Typical. Just my luck.

"I'm sorry," I say, "but how can I help you? I'm about to watch a movie. Have you ever seen *The Prowler*?"

She sniffles as if what I said caused her to cry for some reason. "It's okay," I say. "It's from the eighties and pretty easy to miss."

Silence.

"It has an alternate title... *Rosemary's Killer*... no?"

More silence. Do I hang up here? What the hell is going on?

"The, uh, German release," I say, still unsure about what is happening, "had all of the musical score cut out and replaced with bird noises. Very, um, bizarre. The title of it there was, uh, *Pitchfork of Death*..."

"I'm sorry," she says, her tone quieter, more somber now, almost as if she doesn't care about my movie selection. "I... I lost my husband last week. Not to the virus or anything. But, you know..."

I don't know, but whatever. "I'm sorry to hear that." Now I feel bad.

"It's not... I mean... Sorry. He's... He's in the ground now and... I was going through his closet today and I found something."

Oh no.

"I was wondering," she says, barely above a whisper, "if you could help me."

Anything involving divorce work, or spouses of any kind, I gave up years ago. It was awful and I vowed to never do it again. "I'm sorry, that's not my line of work anymore. I'm not even an investigator anymore. Besides, maybe it's best to just-"

She cuts me off, "It's nothing like that. I didn't find... love letters or anything cliché like that. It's something... else. And I heard you were here and I promise it won't be very hard for you to figure it out. Your reputation precedes you, sir, and if you could find it in your heart to give me just an hour of your time, it would really mean a lot to me."

Well, that sure didn't take long. I don't know how people always seem to find us, but they do. I don't know why I figured this time would be any different. Clients remind me of that weird apparition thing in *It Follows*. No matter where you go, here comes that damn ghost, walkin' right towards you.

"Hold on," I say, getting off the sofa. In the kitchen, I

grab a scrap piece of paper and a Sharpie. "Okay, give me your info. We can give you an hour. Why the hell not?"

Damn it. I have this horrible problem saying no to people who ask me for it. I can't help it. It's the main reason I've kept this line of work up for so long. Even when I moved and didn't have a license anymore, I still wanted to help. And no matter how badly I fool myself into thinking that I'm done... I still want to help. I have no idea who this woman is, and I'm annoyed that she found me... But now that she asked...

Ugh.

I take down her information and tell her we'll be over tomorrow, then I hang up. She failed to mention beforehand that the hour she asked for didn't include the thirty minute drive to get to there and the thirty minute drive back.

ELiSE

Well, here is a twist I wasn't expecting. Not only did Archie vow to never answer his phone again, but he also said he was going to try to go the rest of his life without meeting anyone new. He said he was content with who he knew and wanted to spend the rest of his days focusing on those people and himself and enjoying life. Honestly, I think he just enjoyed the no-hugging, no-closer-than-six-feet-away-at-all-time thing so much that he applied the whole quarantine coda to his everyday life.

We haven't been settled in the house for twenty-four hours, yet here we are, driving a half-hour away from our new home to meet some lady that somehow tracked down his number. He's so annoyed with himself it's almost comical. Usually, when it's just the two of us in a car, we'll listen to loud music and sing along, being dorky and having a blast. Things our kids would never let us get away with if they were in the backseat.

The car ride today is different. The radio is down low, and I swear I can hear Archie mumbling to himself, telling himself he shouldn't have answered that damn phone.

I put my hand on his knee and give it a little pat. "It's okay. It's one person who probably found some note or something that her husband left behind. It'll be no big deal."

"She said it wasn't anything like that."

"You know just as well as I do that clients lie all the time."

They almost literally never tell the truth. We learned that the hard way, and we've applied that knowledge to every case we've had since.

"How did she find us?"

"People always find us. The amount of semi-famous investigators is pretty slim." I giggle at the absolute absurdity of the fact that we are semi-famous investigators. It's like a bad Hallmark movie starring some girl from a long-forgotten sitcom and, as Archie always says, some *square-headed idiot* as her love interest.

It's true, though. All the guys on Hallmark movies look pretty much the same and are completely interchangeable.

"It's never going to stop," Archie says, sighing.

"It'll stop," I say, blatantly lying.

"You're terrible at that."

"Yeah, yeah, I'm not the lying master like you. You should teach a class."

Archie smiles, his good mood returning. "I prefer bullshitter."

I give his knee a little squeeze. "Bullshitter it is. Although that scene you played in the back of the truck yesterday was laughable. *Uh uh, the wall you measured was wrong, uh uh, this is the TV we agreed on, uh uh.*"

Archie laughs.

"Yeah," I say, "pretty lame, babe. Pretty lame, indeed."

The drive to Palm Beach, down the eastern coastline of Florida, was longer than Archie anticipated thanks to an alligator crossing the street and being hit by a car. The story doesn't end there, however. The alligator served as a launching pad for the car, sending it fifteen feet into the air and crashing down on it's side, blocking all lanes of traffic. But I can't say I hated the delay. Despite driving thousands and thousands of miles throughout the last couple of weeks, it was nice to have some time with no farting children or barking dogs.

It took us an hour and a half, one destroyed Bentley, and one pissed-off alligator, to get to Sarah Benson's house. When we arrived, she was sitting on her porch, seemingly waiting for us to arrive. When she recognized us, she got to her feet and came out to greet us.

We parked on the street. Her driveway had two cars parked in it, despite there being a garage. I guess I should say one car and one truck.

"Thank you so much for coming," Sarah says as we're getting out of the car.

Archie shrugs.

"You're welcome," I say, trying to project a little bit more positivity to the situation than my husband.

"Come... Come inside. Please."

I nod, and we follow her through the front door and into her home, a modestly decorated but impeccably cleaned two-bedroom about three miles from the coastline.

Sarah Benson leads us to the sofa and motions for us to take a seat. Archie plops down like he lives here and says, "So, what's up?"

No small talk for him.

"Well," Sarah says before being interrupted.

"Actually," Archie says, "I gotta ask... How did you get our number?"

"Um," Sarah says. If she's offended, she doesn't show it, "the internet."

"Right," Archie says, stretching his arms above his head like he's about to settle in for a nap. "Because we still have the Montana numbers, right?"

"Yeah."

Archie turns to me and mumbles, "We'll need to change those."

I smirk. I have no idea what else to do. Tact and social cues are certainly not my husband's strongest qualities.

"Sorry," I say to Sarah, "please continue."

"I must say," she says to Archie, "you don't look like the fella that played you in the movie."

Archie has heard this a million times, and although he doesn't show it, I can sense his inner fists tightening.

He ignores it.

The petite Sarah sits in an armchair to our left and sighs, the comment still hanging in the air like a raincloud. She's sitting forward, arms rested on her bony knees as if she might have to get up and run away in a hurry.

Archie, already annoyed with how long this is taking, says, "You were saying something about finding... something?"

"Yes... sorry. My husband Carl passed away and I've been keeping myself occupied by cleaning everything. Anything and everything. If it's in this house, I've cleaned it."

I smile and encourage her to continue.

"So, yesterday, after the funeral, I finally decided to do the closets. I haven't decided what to do with Carl's stuff yet, but I figured I could at least organize it." She leans over, grabs a briefcase from beside the chair and places it on the coffee table in front of us.

"That's when I found this."

"What is it?" I ask, genuinely curious now.

Sarah pops the locks and opens the case, revealing stacks and stacks of cash, just like in the movies.

This gets Archie's attention. He was convinced this was another cheating spouse case. "Yowza."

"How much is there?" I ask.

Sarah shakes her head. "I haven't counted. More money than I've ever had in my life, that much is for sure."

"So," Archie says, "I'm confused."

"There is no way my Carl could have earned this. And even if he did, why wouldn't he tell me about it?"

I lean forward towards the case and begin to reach for the money. "Do you mind?"

"No," Sarah says quietly, her arms back on her knees.

I begin removing the bundles of money, one by one. "Have you gone through it?"

Sarah shakes her head no. "I've been too terrified to even touch it."

"Well, I mean, there could be a note or some clue in here, somewhere. I'm just going to look. You never know."

"By all means."

I smile and empty the case. Nothing. "Hmm."

"So," Archie says, leaning back even farther, "what do you want us to do?"

"I need you to find out where it came from. It's not ours. There's no way."

"Did your husband ever do any investing?" I ask. "Any digital currency? My husband did that after the movie came out and it worked out pretty well for us. It's something he could have just been playing around with for fun and stumbled on to something."

Sarah shakes her head again. "No. No way. He never showed any interest in any of that. Honestly, he could barely turn the volume up and down on his phone. Tech-savvy, my husband was not. And, I mean, if it was something like that, I'm the one that handles the finances. I do our taxes. He wouldn't be able to hide it from me. Do you understand?"

"Please don't get offended by this," I say, "but how did he die?"

Another head shake. "I know what you're thinking. It's nothing like that. He was a smoker. A heavy smoker. It caught up to him."

Unless he *heavily*-smoked outside, Sarah has done a great job of cleaning this place. I don't smell any signs of smoke in this house. Archie, however, is cringing at the thought of sitting on a smoke-soaked sofa. He leans forward, turns his head and tries to smell his back.

I pretend that I don't notice. A difficult task when your husband looks like a dog that's trying to fight its own tail.

"So," Archie says, apparently satisfied that his best *Strangers: Prey at Night* t-shirt isn't ruined with the foul stench of smoke, "I still don't understand what you want us to do. Why not go to the police if you think there is something wrong with the money?"

"It's not that I think there is something wrong with it... I know there is something wrong with it. I just need to know... what... exactly."

"Again," Archie says, "take it to the police. I'm sure they'll be able to figure out where a briefcase full of money came from."

"Yeah..." Sarah says, her voice trailing off. "About that. See, the thing is, Mr. and Mrs. Lemons... I need this money. Our savings was drained and I don't have much left. I haven't counted it yet, but I can tell you that it will pay my mortgage for a very, very long time. Do you... *understand* what I'm saying?"

"Not really," I say, although I have an idea.

"I want this money," she says. "I need this money. But... I can not, in good faith, take it if it was... if it does... belong to someone who needs it also."

Archie gives me a look like he thinks Sarah is absolutely out of her mind and we wasted the entire day. I can't say I disagree with him, but there is something so desperate about this woman that I want to help her.

"You want us to find out where it came from," I say, "so you can decide if you would feel right keeping it."

"Does that make me a bad person?"

"Hey," Archie says, getting to his feet, "I've stolen drinks out of suspects' fridges before. And change that was just laying around. I'm not exactly the moral compass you should look to. Just keep the money safe for a few weeks. If no one comes knocking, spend away."

"Please," Sarah says, barely above a whisper. "I just need to know. And I need to know what my husband was up to. If I go to the police, two things would probably happen. They both would include me losing the money... and possibly having Carl's reputation sullied. I just need to know where it came from. If he robbed some multi-billion dollar bank that's insured up the wazoo, and no one was injured, then eff 'em, I'm keeping it. If he conned some little old lady out of her retirement, then I have to give it back...

"Please. I'll pay you whatever I can afford. And even

more... if I keep the money."

"We don't want your money," I say honestly. "I can't promise that this will be our top priority, but we can definitely do some digging around and see what we can find. Do you mind if we take a stack of these bills with us just so we can have the serial numbers? We'll return it, of course."

"Of course. And please. If it makes my Carl look bad-"

"We will tell you and be discreet."

"I have to pay you something."

I shake my head. "I'll tell you what. You can pay us by coming to a performance sometime at the Sunrise Cove Arts Center when we finally open."

"I don't know what that is."

"Well, it's not open yet, but it's a center we founded for live performances, plays, and things like that. We bought an old one-screen theater that closed due to the pandemic and are transforming it into a stage. So, when it's up and running, come see a show. That can be our payment."

With tears in her eyes, Sarah says, "I would love to. That husband of mine never took me anywhere. Wouldn't even go to church with me. Said it was a big waste of time."

"Great. It's a date, then."

We better leave. Archie is so annoyed. His eyes are rolled so far back they're about to snap the optic nerves connected to his brain.

"Thank you," Sarah says, breathing a sigh of relief.

Typically, I would offer to shake her hand, but times are still a little weird, so I just smile. "We'll be in touch, but like I said, it might be pretty slow going. Do you have enough money to get by for a while?"

Sarah nods. "Yes, I'm okay for now. I will probably sell Carl's truck soon, too... So, if you know anyone that needs a 2001 Dodge Ram..."

"If I find anyone, I'll let you know. Okay... Stay strong, and I'm so sorry for the world's loss of your husband."

Tears again, this time streaming. "That's very kind of you to say. Thank you."

"Hold on," I say, thinking of one last question. "Did your husband go anywhere in the weeks leading up to his death? I mean... Was he bedridden?"

"He was bedridden the last week or so, but before that, he would get up and watch TV on the sofa."

"But he never left the house?"

"He went to a support group on a fairly regular schedule."

"When was the last time he left alone?"

"A week before he got really bad, so two weeks. Another meeting, then right back home. I offered to go, but... they're for people that are dying."

I nod. "Yeah. And what about before that. He had a job, I assume."

"Of course. My Carl was a security guard at a hotel."

"Do you mind if I ask which hotel?"

"Ocean Sands. It's one of the major hotels down along the water - a resort, not just a hotel. I know what you're thinking, though. I loved him, but he could never pull off an embezzling scam. Believe me, I wish he had. Stealing from a major business that charged tourists hundreds and hundreds of dollars a night while only paying him fifteen dollars an hour, well, I would sleep just fine knowing that."

Instead of telling her that I've seen men do some shocking things, bad things, I just smile and nod and say goodbye again.

She's fighting back the tears once again as she waves goodbye.

"See ya later," Archie says as we make our way towards the street, Sarah closing the door and locking it behind us.

In the car, Archie looks at me and asks, "So, whattaya think?"

I purse my lips together tightly and shrug like an idiot. I have absolutely no idea. This makes Archie laugh.

"Yeah, me either. We should buy this truck, though. She's a beast!"

"What for?"

"Uh, because it's awesome."

"It looks like a gigantic piece of crap," I say. "I peeked in the side window. Babe, the dash is being held together with duct tape."

"So... who needs a... dash?"

"Mm-hmm..."

"C'mon, Elise. Wouldn't it be awesome to have some gigantic piece of crap? You could do whatever you wanted with it. You could literally crash into shopping carts with it at the grocery store and not even care. How many times have you gone to turn into a parking space and there is a goddamn cart right in the way? Before, you would worry about it, maybe go to a different space, but not with this. Not with this monster. Just pull in and shove that stupid cart right into a tree!"

"We're not buying this."

"This isn't over!" Archie says, way too over-dramatically. "Not by a long shot! You'll rue the day you told me I couldn't buy this gigantic turd."

"You don't even know what rue means," I say, laughing at this performance he's putting on.

"Rue McClanahan!"

ARCHiE

I can't believe some kook not only found my number but called on the exact day we finished moving in. How does that even happen? I mean, the odds of that should be astronomical. And all because our crappy movie played in some theaters during a global pandemic. Thanks a lot, Covid Bat!

Well, on the plus side, it's not like this case requires much effort. Honestly, we could just sit on it for two weeks then say the money is in the clear and everyone is happy. The odds of the money being stolen from a little old lady are slim to none. I've worked for little old ladies before, and my biggest payday was eleven cents and a day-old cinnamon roll.

The cinnamon roll and the change went into the gutter on my way out to my car.

This is a true story.

Anyway, my point is, this lady should just take the money and shut up. As long as she didn't steal it, she has deniability, and honestly, if no one has come looking for it yet, they're not going to. Her husband is dead. There's no proof she ever even saw the money.

Oh well. Can't convince some people, I suppose.

"Can we stop somewhere?" Elise says.

"Sure. Where?"

"I don't know. Coffee place? I could go for a tropical tea."

"Sure. Just not Starbucks."

"Believe me, I know your rule."

My rule is no Starbucks ever, under any condition. There is no real reason aside from me being a crotchety old man that doesn't want to give his money to a global monopoly that makes crappy coffee.

Edgy, right?

I know. I'm embarrassed by it, too, but whatever.

Elise laughs. "I'll find a place."

She pulls out her phone and presumably looks for a place to stop. I've never been down here before, so I'm enjoying the new scenery. No snow in sight. Glorious.

"There's a place about a mile up."

"Okey-dokey."

"Oh my god!" Elise says in a tone that suggests either shock or repulsion. Or maybe a little of both.

"What? God, what?"

"I just opened Reddit and look what popped up. Literally just opened it."

I glance towards her phone and see spread-apart male butt cheeks and a sagging punching bag dangling below.

I want to drive my car into the ocean.

"What is wrong with people?!" Elise yells. "God!"

"That's just on Reddit?"

"Frontpage!"

"That's sexual assault! How is that even allowed? That's no different than some guy opening his trench coat and showing you his dong."

"I'm done. I'm social media free from here on out."

Elise swipes her phone a few times, and I see her delete the entire app. "Good riddance."

"I won't be sleeping tonight."

"Ugh, so gross. Take a left at the light."

We walk into Smitty's Beach House, a small coffee shop located a block from the beach, and get in line. I knew Florida has always been known as a little kooky, but here's something I never thought I'd see.

I nudge Elise and tell her to look.

There is a lady seated at the far table, near the window. On her table, a hedgehog is licking coffee from the lid of her cup.

A hedgehog!

"That's the most wholesome thing I've ever seen," Elise says, seeming to mean it. I want to run out screaming. If this kind of behavior is allowed in full view of the public, what the hell is going on in the kitchen?!

Florida, man. Florida

We get our teas, and instead of getting back in the car, we decide to sit on the patio and enjoy the view for a bit. There is a TV playing the news, which is literally the last thing anyone would want to watch while sipping a drink and looking out at the ocean.

I can't help but watch. Nothing important. Apparently, the top story on the local Palm Beach news is the disappearance of an infamous gangster off the coast. His boat was found, but not him. He hasn't been seen since a warrant was finally issued for his arrest. For what, I have no idea. Nor do I care. Although being as we're in the land of table hedgehogs, I can only imagine what kind of shenanigans this supposed gangster was up to.

And please... Gangsters. They're not even real. What a bunch of phonies.

"You watching this?" Elise says, even though I'm clearly watching it.

"I want to meet this so-called gangster. So dumb."

"Gangsters are dumb?"

"Totally. Like, mobsters. Like that's even a real thing."

"Um, didn't you watch *The Sopranos*? And haven't you seen *Casino* like a million times?"

"Yeah, Elise. Fiction."

"I'm pretty sure those are both rooted in fact."

"Sure, Elise. Maybe back in the 1800s, but not today."

"The 1800s? What are you talking about? Half the Florida coast is mob-run. You have to realize that."

"Hey, lame."

Elise rolls her eyes at me. "Ooookay."

I have a feeling she believes I could be mistaken.

"You've been to Las Vegas, right? I mean, you realize where that came from, right?"

"Fine, sure. The mob, oohhhhh, scary."

Elise mumbles something I can't quite make out. No worries. I've already lost interest and am back to enjoying my ocean view and ninety-nine percent humidity.

Little warm. Not gonna lie. Little warm.

"What the..."

About fifteen yards away, down on the beach, a man with a mullet and handlebar mustache, dressed in a full-on karate gi complete with a black belt, is yelling at a pink flamingo.

"What the hell," Elise says, turning her full attention towards the strange mulleted man.

Mullet Man yells, "I've about had it with you, you sumbitch!"

The flamingo squawks. They're almost standing nose to nose, and I've never wanted to see a fight this badly before in my life.

It really does appear that the flamingo is taunting him.

"What the hell are you doing?" Elise yells to the man.

Mullet Man turns and yells back, "This son of a bitch is sleeping with my wife!"

Elise tries to contain her laughter, but it doesn't work. She literally snorts.

"Did you hear him?" Mullet Man yells. "Son of a bitch just called me a punk! He-ya!" He assumes a fighting stance, legs staggered, arms up, fists clenched.

Oh my god, oh my god.

The flamingo is still talkin' trash when Mullet Man roundhouse kicks it straight in the face. It sounds like two coconut halves being clapped together

"No mercy!" Mullet Man yells as the flamingo is staggering backward.

Elise and I are struck silent by the unbelievable events unfolding before us.

The flamingo regains its footing and comes charging at Mullet Man with pure rage. It leads with a head-butt, followed by several bites from its long beak. Now it is Mullet Man who is stunned. He staggers backward into some brush, and goes down. More flamingos join the fight.

Mullet Man emerges from the brush and runs towards the street, an angry mob of flamingos hot on his tail. His screams linger long after we lose sight of him.

Elise and I stare at each other wide-eyed. We're both laughing so hard we are crying.

Florida, man.

After a solid ten minutes of trying to regain our calm, Elise says, "So what are we going to do about this money?"

I let out an overly-dramatic sigh and say I don't know. "Do you have those bills on you, or did you leave them in the car?"

"They're in my purse." She pulls them out and hands them to me.

"The hundreds are blue, so it's not like it was some long-forgotten robbery. Where the hell is the date on these things now?"

Elise points to show me.

2017.

"Okay, so I guess we search for any robberies involving a large sum of money from 2017 to the present. If we find anything, we cross-check it with Sarah and see if we can place her husband there."

"Sounds easy enough," Elise says, returning the bills to her bag.

"I should hope so since you said we would be working for free."

"Oh stop, we don't need the money right now and you know it. That poor woman is struggling. We are not. Pay it forward."

Someone paid it forward to me in a drive-thru once. All I ordered was a ninety-nine-cent soft-serve cone. Still, I felt pressured into paying it forward again and ended up buying some assholes behind me a forty-dollar

Burger King meal. From then on out, the pay it forward stops with me.

I finish my tea and say, "Fine," then stand up and chuck my cup in the trash. "Let's get out of here, babydoll."

"Oh baby," Elise says, linking her arm in mine as we head back to the car.

Just as I press the little button on the door handle to unlock the car, a man with cutoff jean shorts and a sleeveless Big Johnson shirt runs up to me, literally runs, stopping just short of my face, and yells, *yells*, "You wanna buy some meth?!"

What planet are we on?!

Elise and I quickly get in the car and shut the doors.

"I said!" he yells while crawling on our hood, both his palms now flat on my windshield. He's gazing in at us with dead eyes, "what about some crackety crack crack?!"

I look to Elise, who is staring at the guy, mouth open, in complete shock.

I yell back to him, "I think the My Pillow Guy is in town! Go ask him!"

"K bye!" the man yells, rolling off the hood of our car.

"Guaranteed sale!" I yell back as he scampers off into some trees and out of our lives forever. "Also look for a guy in a karate costume!"

He doesn't hear me.

Elise and I share a look of utter disbelief.

"See," I say, "if we had that truck, we could have just plowed right through that guy."

ELiSE

I should have asked that Big Johnson guy in the Daisy Dukes if he had any weed. Florida is one of those states that allows everything except marijuana, which is so ass-backward it's almost mind-blowing, considering the amount of drugs they have coming in from the Caribbean, Cuba, wherever.

I mean, it's okay... All that means is I won't have to pay taxes on it when I do buy it. And something tells me it won't be too hard to find elsewhere until I get my medicinal recommendation from some online quack doctor, thus making my purchasing of it totally legal.

See, ass-backward.

"The more I think about it," I say as we pass the *Welcome to Sunrise Cove* sign, "I don't think the money came from Carl's job."

"Nah," Archie says. "No way. People who embezzle a hundred thousand dollars don't go withdraw it from the ATM and keep it in a suitcase. It may have come from someone in the hotel, but not the hotel itself."

"And if it did come from someone in the hotel, why has no one reported it. If it was stolen out of a room, security and maids would be the first people questioned. No, something is off here. I mean, we could be wrong. But as of now, I don't think it's the Ocean Sands's money."

"Totes," Archie says, pulling on to our street, where I see something I haven't seen in a very long time, and it makes my heart swell. The boys are outside playing. And not just the boys - everyone.

That loud mix of laughter and screaming - the sound of pure joy, of an innocent childhood summer, reminds me of when I was a kid before everything turned to shit. I had one or two good summers, when Grandma and Grandpa did their best to make the school-free months, especially the Fourth of the July, the best it could be.

Looking back on it now, though, I can see the cracks in the armor; the bitter stares from my grandpa, the late-night fights when they thought no one was awake. Maybe I am just romanticizing the few times in my youth when I wasn't completely miserable and turning it into something much more.

I suppose none of that matters, anymore. Not going to lie, though. I'm tempted to run out in the street with these kids and join the game.

I'm going to make this the best Fourth of July ever. For them. And for me. We've all earned it.

The three years we lived in Montana, I barely saw these kids move, aside from skateboarding on a ramp Archie built, but even that didn't last very long. The winters were long and tedious, and a lot of craptastic horror movies were watched while sitting stagnant on a sofa that got so much use we had to buy a new one a few months ago.

My best friend Jamie is sitting in a lawn chair, Gary's Pack'n'Play set up next to her. They're watching the game of... actually, I have no idea what game they are playing. Eric has a baseball and just threw it up in the air as high as he could over to a cluster of kids. They're all fighting to catch it.

Hey, I don't care what the game is as long as they're happy!

After we came into our big payday, we bought the first four houses on Wahoo St. in a new neighborhood called Bodfish Bay. I've told you this already, but the thought of leaving our friends behind in Montana was unbearable to me, so we brought everyone along. Our house is the first, Jamie's is next door, Liz and Monica, Eric's best friend Milo's parents, are next to her. At the end, Elliot's best friend Brioni, her sister Reese, and mom Tabitha. It's like I moved into Fantasyland. It's perfect.

"Hey hey!" Jamie says, coming to greet us. "How'd it go?"

Archie grunts, "Some lady found a suitcase full of money and is having moral problems spending it. Apparently, her moral problems are now my problem. I swear to god..."

Jamie laughs and puts her arm on Archie's shoulder. "You gonna be okay, big guy?"

"He'll be fine," I say, smacking him on the butt. "Right?"

"Yeah, yeah. Should be easy enough."

"How did she find you?" Jamie asks, clearly enjoying Archie's grumpiness.

"Dude," he says, removing his sweat-drenched Dodgers hat and flailing his arms like this is the most baffling mystery in the history of mysteries, "who knows."

"Archie!" Brioni yells as she comes running from the street to give my husband a hug. This cheers him up immediately.

Brioni is Elliot's little girlfriend. She absolutely adores Archie, especially since her own dad pretty much ditched out on her whole family a little while back.

"Hey, kid!" Archie says, wrapping his arm around her shoulders. The feeling is mutual. Brioni latches on to him and squeezes tight.

Yeah, buying these four houses was the best thing we could have done with that money.

"Come on, guys, let's get ready for tonight." Since it's our first full day all moved in, we decided to have a little party in the backyard, just for us. On top of all that, there is a scheduled rocket launch from Cape Canaveral in t-minus three hours, and we have the perfect view.

The dinner was more successful than the launch, which got scrapped with nine seconds left on the countdown clock, but that's okay. They'll do it again, and it'll give us another excuse to have another backyard party.

After dinner, Jamie, Liz, Monica, Tabitha, and myself, gathered around the kitchen table for our typical squawk session. Gary is crapped out in his little chair next to us, and the kids, dogs, and Archie are all in the other room watching a movie with an awful lot of stabbing noises and screams.

"You guys want to hear something embarrassing?" Tabitha says.

"Duh," Liz says with a smile.

"I only bring this up because of the news lately, but you know that mob guy that's missing at sea, apparently?"

"Oh, dang," I say. "We just saw that on the news today. Archie doesn't seem to believe in the mob for some reason."

Everyone chuckles, myself included.

"Well," Tabitha continues, "do you know anything about him?"

"Not a thing."

"Okay, so yeah, he's some East Coast mob guy. I don't know much about him personally. Don't care, really, but apparently he has been untouchable for decades and he's been like a ghost, basically. Well, they finally got something they can bust him on and it's so rinky-dink that it's almost laughable. Still, it is *something*. And, if the feds get this, then they'll hopefully have him in prison and, I dunno, start linking him to past crimes, or something like that. I don't know. That's not what my story is really about, anyway."

"What are they trying to get him on?"

Tabitha's face flushes bright red. "Multi-level marketing scams."

"Like, pyramid schemes?" Monica asks.

"Exactly. I guess he sort of retired from the whole mob thing and was planning on going out undefeated. No arrests. That was going to be his big claim to fame, despite a ton of horrible crimes that nobody could seem to prove. So he started Fat Killer."

"Fat Killer?" I say. "Subtle."

"Right?" Tabitha says, clearly still embarrassed. "I fell for it, though. I mean, it seemed like it was a sure-fire thing."

"So what's illegal about it?"

"Apparently none of these products are of any real worth. They're crap, basically, and the money comes from finding more suckers to peddle the crap."

"Where does he get the product?"

"I'm sure it's just garbage repackaged. I'm not positive, though. Probably stuff bought in wholesale from like Bulgaria or something.

"Anyway, all that is bad enough, and the FTC has been cracking down on these MLM companies anyway, and you know the FBI was desperate to find him. So, when Fat Killer started making claims that their vitamins could help prevent infection from Covid, that's when they decided to strike. It doesn't seem like much, but it's a hefty enough no-no to at least bring him in and hold him for a while. A long while, hopefully."

"Didn't they lock up Al Capone for like mail fraud or something like that?" Liz says.

"I think it was tax evasion," I say, although I'm not entirely sure. "I know Bernie Madoff and that Ponzi guy got charged with mail fraud."

Archie, cutting through the kitchen towards the fridge, says, "Ehhhhhh," and gives us two thumbs up.

"I said Ponzi, dork, not Fonzie."

"Ehh," Archie says, sad this time. His thumbs are now down.

"What are you guys watching in there?"

"*Pool Party Massacre,*" Archie says, way too enthusiastically.

"Right," Jamie giggles, "it's up for all those Oscars."

"Psh, it should be."

Laughing, I say, "No dudes allowed. Take a hike."

Archie shrugs, "I'm just getting a drink. Calm down, ladies, calm down."

Archie refills his cup and then walks back to the

living room. Halfway there, he yells, "K bye!" and takes off running into the other room. Everyone laughs, but nobody but me gets the joke.

"Anyway," I say, "with those rinky-dink cases, sometimes you have to take what you can get, I guess."

"So why is this embarrassing, Tab?" Monica says.

"Because," Tabitha grunts, "when we were stuck in quarantine and we were excited about the move, I got suckered into his stupid scam. See, you girls aren't on social media, so I was able to post and keep it a secret, at least from you guys. So embarrassing."

"How'd it work out for you?" Liz asks.

"How do you think? It was awful. I was suckered into it by some dumb girl I went to high school with a million years ago who literally used to call me Fatty Fat Fat. She completely manipulated me into joining. Gave me some spiel about me being a single parent and having extra income and just dog shit after dog shit until I finally just said okay. I swear to god, if I ever see that girl, I am punching her square in her giant, horse teeth. Special delivery from Fatty Fat Fat, bitch! Kapow!"

Tab Popeye-punches the invisible high school girl to really drive the point home.

Sometimes when I'm bored or can't sleep, I watch anti-MLM videos on YouTube, so I know all about this, how the product is basically useless, but you have to recruit more and more people just for the one percent chance of making money. They teach you how to find something about a potential mark and exploit it.

I used to get hit up for it all the time when I was single, and they really do use any and every tactic to get you to sign up. That's all that matters to them, and it sucks.

I'm happy to say I never got involved, but at times it was tempting, just from the way they try to sell it. And for a runaway girl from New York with a GED and not much else, who grew up dirt poor and on welfare, the idea of having disposable income was like a dream. I just couldn't risk it, though.

I made the right choice. I've heard their tactics have become far more sinister since my days of social media. I've even heard them going so far as exploiting people's children or diseases, or anything really, just to make a sale. I'm sure that, along with the false claims, have something to do with the FCA cracking down on them.

Oh well. Things turned out pretty well for me, and I'm glad I never did it, but I can totally understand the allure if you don't know all the facts.

"Are you still doing it?" I ask.

Tab shakes her head. "No! No way. It was awful."

"So, lesson learned. That's not embarrassing."

"It is to me. I hope they catch that guy and throw him in jail forever. His bullshit products suck. What was I thinking; Saran Wrap that dissolves fat? God!" She face-palms herself.

"Yeah," Jamie says, laughing. "That's pretty bad."

Tabitha looks up, trying to keep a straight face. "I hate you so much."

We all share a laugh before Tabitha says, "I hope they throw all of them in jail, especially that bitch that duped me. Enjoy your weight loss journey in prison, *bitch!*"

More laughter.

"That bitch posted a photo on Instagram the other day of her working on her flat-ass booty, and in the background, her dumb cuck husband was sitting at his desk, totally staged, trying to work, but he was too distracted by her luscious flapjack ass. It was the most cringe photograph I've ever seen in my life. I feel so bad for the husband. I'm sure he wishes he was dead."

Everyone laughs again.

Between this, my husband, my pups, and all the kids, I've never been happier.

Talk about a dream - I'm living one.

ARCHiE

"Archie, guess what?" Elise says to me while shaking me awake. "Guess what we're doing tomorrow night?"

I have no idea what's going on. "Huh?"

"Jamie just texted me."

"So? She lives next door. Go back to bed."

"It's ten o'clock, babe."

I open my eyes. Elise is not in bed next to me like I initially thought. She's standing in front of me, fully clothed. "Really?"

"Yes, really. So guess what?"

"I don't know. What?"

"Tomorrow night... Jamie said she found a little restaurant, slash bar, slash whatever, called The Gull, where they do live-band karaoke and do you know what tomorrow night's theme is?"

"Meth?"

She laughs then tells me to shut up. "It's nineties night! I swear to god! We're totally going."

"I'm not doing karaoke. Have we met?"

"We'll discuss your participation later on, but you're definitely going. Nineties night! You're the biggest nineties fan ever! And with a live band backing you. Come on. This is why we moved to Florida, for some fun. And don't act like you don't want to get up on stage, in front of a band, and sing 'Teenage Dirtbag' or one of those other horrible songs you love so much – 'Breakfast at Tiffany's,' or 'Sex and Candy.'

"Those are all great songs!" I say, almost genuinely offended.

"So go back to sleep if you want, do whatever you've gotta do, but tomorrow night at six pm, you have plans."

She bounces up and down a few times then

practically skips out of the room. I close my eyes and fall back asleep.

"Hey there, Rip Van Winkle," Elise says to me when I finally come stumbling out of the bedroom at around noon. "Or, since we're in Florida, I should say Robert Van Winkle?"

Robert Van Winkle - VIP Florida native Vanilla Ice's real name. "Funny girl."

"You love me."

"No doubt about it. Man, I guess the move finally caught up with me. I could not get out of bed today."

"Yeah, we noticed." She's sitting at the kitchen table, her laptop open in front of her.

"Nice shirt."

It's plain black with the word MOOCH written in huge white letters across the front. She's tried convincing me that being a mooch is nothing to be proud of, but I beg to differ. It's gotten me far in life.

"Thanks. Where are the kids?"

"Gary is sleeping, and Eric and Elliot are at Milo's. Listen closely. You'll be able to hear them."

"Why are they always so loud?"

Elise shrugs. "Boys."

"I guess. What are you doing?"

"Looking up robberies, trying to trace that money."

"Any luck?"

"For that amount? No. But good lord. I did a broad search of crimes just from the past three years; listen to what I came up with. These are all within a one-hundred-mile radius of us. You ready?"

"I'm ready."

"Okay. The first one isn't really a crime, but it's still fascinating nonetheless. *Thousands of gun owners in Florida plan to shoot down Hurricane Maxine.*"

"Oh god. Did it work?"

"Well, I don't remember hearing about Hurricane Maxine, so you do the math. Here, I'm just going to list off some more. Prepare yourself."

"I feel like nothing can prepare me."

"Here we go. *Florida man denies drinking and driving. Swears he only drank at stop signs.*

"*Florida man arrested for assaulting girlfriend with fried chicken.*"

"Jesus."

"*Florida man stabs tourist despite having no arms.*

"*Florida man gives* exonerating *dashcam video following traffic accident, accidentally includes video of him robbing convenient store.*"

"These aren't true. They can't be."

"Archie, a guy ran up to you and tried to sell you meth with the enthusiasm of a Girl Scout trying to sell her very first box of cookies. They're real and they're spectacular. I promise."

"Please continue."

"*Florida man steals thirty-three-thousand dollars in rare coins – cashes them in at Coinstar machine for twenty-nine dollars.*

"*Florida man pulls out plastic badge and tells speeding motorcyclist,* I the police.

"*Florida man gives police fake name to try and avoid arrest. Fake name wanted for murder.*

"*Florida man leaves strip club drunk, crashes into nearby house, manages to run himself over.*"

"My heart can't take any more of these. Please. Make it stop."

Elise is laughing so hard she's about to cry. "One more. "*Florida man tries to steal dozens of birds from pet store, disguised with plastic bag over his head, ends up suffocating himself.*"

I can feel brain cells dying. "Did we make the right decision moving here?"

"I think this is the best decision we've ever made, actually."

I laugh. "You could be right. Ya know what else, I think that Sarah lady should just keep the money, and we retire for good."

"Ha. Maybe. But, I don't know. Something about

this money is intriguing to me. Like, remember the news yesterday about the mob guy that's missing. What if her husband was secretly involved with the mafia? Ya think?"

I sigh. "No, I don't think. Even if the mob is real, like you seem to think, if the movies have taught me anything, it's that that's not how the mob works, so you're way off base on that one."

"That literally makes no sense."

She's right. Busted. I laugh again, then shrug. Whatever.

"Like, what were you going for there?" Elise asks, stupefied by the terribleness of my lie. "Are you trying to make me think the mob doesn't use... money?"

"Look, I know it wasn't my best work."

"Downright embarrassing." She's laughing now. "Pretty sure that's gaslighting, too."

"It's not gaslighting. It was just terrible, regular ol' lying."

"I think that's gaslighting, too." She's clearly enjoying this.

"I just don't want to do this."

"That's fine," she says, her smile so wide and cheerful. "You don't have to. I'm capable of doing it."

"Of course you are. You're better than me."

"Let's not get crazy here, Mr. Famous."

"Dumbbbbbb."

"It's true."

"If I'm famous, then you're famous, too."

Still smiling brightly, she closes her laptop with a quick flick of her hand, and says, "Never said I wasn't."

It's the most beautiful smile I've ever seen in my life and I know that there will never be a case, or anything for that matter, that I don't want to be right next to her.

Forever.

Which, I guess, includes Nineties Night at The Gull.

—

ELISE

Archie agreed to go to karaoke, which makes me insanely happy. I know he won't sing anything, but that's okay. Archie likes the least amount of attention humanly possible. Whenever we were on the news, he would blend into the background and let me do all the talking. So, getting him on stage, under a spotlight, would be a monumental task that probably won't happen anytime soon.

I'd probably have better chances of getting him to dance in front of a crowd. And not a slow dance – a dance dance.

He would be equally mortified by either.

This has nothing to do with anything, but sometimes, when it's just Archie and me, I'll start my own little dance party. Just for fun. Sometimes just to make him a little uncomfortable, sometimes just because I feel like dancing. So, if you ever see me with my arms up, shaking my hips in front of my husband, who is clearly embarrassed, you'll know why.

All in good fun, though.

One day he'll dance with me. And one day he'll sing me a song.

Just not tomorrow.

But!

You know who might do a little ditty up on that stage?

Me!

I'm just about to text Jamie back and tell her the good news when a breaking news alert pops up on my screen. "Holy shit. Archie!"

Archie comes sauntering back into the room and asks what's up?

"The mob guy. The one from the news yesterday. The one Tabitha was literally just talking about last night..."

"Yeah, what about him?"

"His name was Frank Giuseppe, but his nickname was Mongo."

"Was?"

"He just washed up on the shore."

"On the shore where?"

"Here!"

"Sunrise Cove?"

"Yes!"

"Here two goddamn days and we've got bodies washing up on shore." He's rubbing his eyes so hard I'm afraid they're going to pop. "Typical."

"This is big."

"Great. Just what we wanted."

I read the article, holding a finger up to Archie, telling him to give me a second. Tabitha was right. He's seemingly been a ghost for quite some time. The article says Mongo came down south from New York after a few mob wars forced him out of his home state and into southern Florida. According to this, there was an attempt on his life a few times down here, but I guess that never panned out. Obviously, the FBI has been on to him for a while for various mob-related misdoings but has never been able to bust him. They've never even formally arrested him. They could never hold him.

"You know who Mongo was?" Archie says.

"Yeah, this guy."

"No no. Mongo was one of the bad guys on a horrible old Nickelodeon game show called *Nick Arcade*."

"Must have missed that one."

"It was on in the nineties for a while. It was terrible. Four kids were probably plucked from their parents while on vacation at Universal and forced to play this half-assed game where they're asked ridiculously easy questions that they're too stupid to even get right.

"I remember the host asked which movie has Darth

Vader. One of the kids answered *Space Track*. It was awful. And the host would make up these terrible raps and it was just, ugh. We should watch it."

"Sounds like a date. Anyway, Tabitha told me that they were going to bust this guy on some scam with multi-level marketing. She said it was rinky-dink stuff but they didn't care. They could build more and more cases against him when they finally had him behind bars. Or something like that. She didn't know all the details."

"But now he's dead. Too bad."

"I bet he got whacked!" I say, a little too excitedly.

"Whacked? Come on. By who? A bunch of Surf Body women that lost their two hundred dollars? Get real."

"You never know! And it wasn't Surf Body, it was Fat Killer, although I'm sure that one is just as crooked. There's another one out there called *It's Great!*. Girls used to try to get me to sign up for that one all the time, back in the day. It's another weight loss one that was being pitched to me by girl's I went to Jr. High with who used to make fun of me for being too skinny. So, yeah. The business model isn't exactly rock solid for these companies."

"The name of the company is *It's Great!?*"

"Yeah," I say, trying not to giggle.

"That's just... ridiculous. Like when a used car salesman tells you to trust him."

"That's beside the point."

"And the mob's is named Fat Killer? Hilarious."

"I know, right? Anyway... Look, Mongo's body was so waterlogged and bloated the skin was sliding off him when the paramedics loaded him up. They're totally going to do an autopsy ASAP. Just watch. How exciting."

"That would be kinda cool to see. I mean, his skin falling off. How can they even identify him if he's so messed up? I'm guessing a career mob fella like him wouldn't just be walking into the ol' Family Dentistry on Cyprus St. to have his teeth cleaned. "

"Yeah, it didn't mention anything about dental

records. Hold on... It says further tests will be performed, but authorities believe it to be the body of, yada yada yada, based on appearance, a ring he always wore, and a distinguishable tattoo on his chest. It says here that he has a brother that moved out west thirty years ago, and a sister that's locked up in New Jersey, and probably several kids, but nobody knows who or where they are. There is a picture of his corpse if you want to see."

"Duh."

"Fair warning. It's pretty gross."

Archie shrugs.

I show him the picture, Mongo's lifeless, swollen body on the shore of our quiet little beach town.

"Oof," Archie says, "bloated is an understatement. He's worse than one of those terrible J.K. Rowling mysteries."

"Right? There's more to this, though. I promise. Just wait and see."

"You know the ones... the ones where she pretends to be a man writing. She doesn't even get her own irony with her hate-fueled comments."

"Yeah," I say, "I got it. Focus, babe. We're not talking about J.K. Rowling, right now. We're talking about the dead man that washed ashore."

"Does this affect my dinner or TV?"

"Why would it?"

"Fantastic."

He's hangry and now he's thinking about J.K. Rowling. That's never a good combination.

I try not to laugh. The things my husband gets worked up about. I swear.

Hilarious.

"Wait," I say as we're walking into the kitchen. "How did you know he was a career mob guy?"

Archie laughs. "Maybe I did a little digging. I don't know. I don't remember. I'm hungry."

"Oh. I see. So... you do believe in the mob?"

"Maybe. I don't recall."

46

I give him a playful punch in the arm.

"Fine," he says. "Maybe the mob is real."

"Maybe."

"And those J.K Rowling mysteries do suck. Seven-hundred-and-fifty pages for a detective novel! Get the hell out of here. Two-hundred-and-twenty-seven pages is the maximum! Anything more than that and the book sucks."

I try not to laugh. This makes no sense at all. "Come on, babe, let me get you some food."

Absolutely hilarious.

The kids went to bed an hour ago, and Archie has managed to fall asleep next to me in the most ridiculous position I've ever seen. And he wonders why his neck and back always hurt.

Anyway, I decide to take this opportunity to do a little digging on the body of Frank Giuseppe, AKA Mongo. I can't find anything but the same information written thirty different ways.

Too bad.

But this isn't over. I can feel it in my bones.

Eventually, I drag Archie to bed and I drift off. When I awaken, I remember that it's Nineties Night!

Instant good mood!

ARCHiE

It turns out that Nineties Night is an all-age event, so of course the kids wanted to go. All of them. There are so many of us going we had to take three cars, but whatever. At least it's something to do that isn't being snowed in at our house, twiddling our thumbs, and staring at the TV...

Not that I have any objections to staring at the TV.

Anyway, The Gull is a pretty cool place. Not right on the beach, but close enough, it's bigger than I expected, and the crowd is pretty decent. It reminds me of one of those old House of Blues that used to be everywhere but kind of disappeared.

The restaurant, bar, and stage are all in the same room, so the atmosphere was busy and a little chaotic. But, after so long with absolutely zero get-togethers, I can't say I hate it.

We end up rearranging three tables towards the back and sitting together. Jamie and Elise are already up by the stage, flipping through the catalog of songs the live band can play.

The other women and the kids hang back with me, perhaps a little less ambitious than my wife and her best friend. Elise was born for the stage, so I can't imagine how excited she is.

I'm driving the boys and Elise and Jamie home, so those two are taking advantage of the situation. They moved from the side of the stage to the bar, where I see them each down a shot that I'm willing to bet my savings on they did not have to pay for.

The lights go down, and a spotlight comes up. It's following a good-looking woman with the curliest, most awesome hair I've ever seen in my life. After taking the stage, she introduces herself as Roberta, and welcomes us all to Nineties Night at The Gull.

The crowd cheers. The place has been open all day, so everyone has had more than enough time to get happily tipsy.

She tells us if we want to sing, we need to come up as soon as possible and pick a song because the slots fill up quickly.

Elise runs over to me and whispers into my ear that she is fourth and Jamie is fifth. She kisses me on the cheek then runs back to the bar.

I can't wait.

The stage lights rise and the curtain opens, revealing the house band. More drunken cheers from the crowd. An overweight bald man takes the stage slowly, looking like he might throw up. He takes the microphone from the stand, doesn't address the crowd at all, clears his throat then takes a deep breath.

I'm rooting for this guy so much!

The thin woman with long blond hair, sitting behind the drums, claps her sticks together three times and the band comes to life playing *Wonderwall*.

Of course.

The bald man misses his first cue but quickly recovers and goes on to do a not-too-terrible rendition of the Oasis megahit.

The next guy sounds like someone is slowly torturing a cat. Still, he's giving it his all and delivering a version of *Walkin' on the Sun* that I never thought I wanted to hear, but absolutely love. He's also drunk as a skunk, which somehow makes it even better.

That's the fun of karaoke. Sometimes the worst is the best.

After that, *Semi-Charmed Life* is sung decently by a guy that looks like he grew a terribly thin mustache in the nineties and kept it exactly the same from then on out.

The band takes a quick water break, then Elise takes the stage and grabs the mic. She's wearing cut-off shorts, black Converse, and a twenty-year-old

Dashboard Confessional shirt that comes down to the bottom of her ribcage, revealing her tanned stomach. She was never one to be pale, even in a Montana winter... She's already got the beach girl vibe going for her.

She is glowing.

"Hi everybody. My name is Elise Lemons. We just moved here and couldn't be happier."

The crowd cheers and Elise takes it in.

From a little girl, she always wanted to be on the stage, and after three-in-a-row from paunchy white dudes, the crowd is obviously happy to have her.

"So, my husband is in the crowd," she says into her microphone. "Right over there." She points to me. People look, and I want to hide under the table. I'm pretty sure a couple people even booed.

"And, one thing about my husband is that he *loooooves* the nineties, so this is quite the treat for us. So, Archie, love of my life, this one... is for you."

The blonde claps her drumsticks together again, and the band fires up, playing a song I wasn't expecting at all. Where the previous songs were poppy, this is fast. I know it, but I can't believe it's being played here, in a weird restaurant in a small town.

And even more than that, I can't believe the band even knows the song. I can't believe anyone knows this song outside of punk rock fans around the age of forty.

She's Gone is my favorite song on one of my favorite punk albums of the 90's – NOFX's White Trash, Two Heebs, and a Bean. And here it is, being sung so well by my wife, it's about to make me cry like a little baby.

It's a fast song, a serious song, lacking the playfulness of other NOFX songs, and it's absolutely killer.

All the kids turn in unison and look at me, their eyes wide, their jaws dropped.

The crowd is in shock by how loud it is. In fact, it takes them a good thirty seconds before they remember where they are and start giving Elise the praise she

—

deserves.

Her voice is amazing.

The band is amazing.

I had no idea. I am absolutely blown away.

When the song ends she drops the mic, like the superstar she is, throws her arms in the air and takes in the crowd. Jamie runs up on stage after her and almost tackles her with a hug. I'm on my feet, making as much noise as possible.

Pretty sure somebody just booed at me again, though. Not sure what that's all about.

Jamie picks up the mic from the stage floor and the crowd's cheers lower to let her talk. "How about my best friend?" she says, the cheers returning to their previous level.

When the noise dies down, she continues, "So, like I said, that's my best friend. And on top of being ridiculously talented, she also has the biggest heart of any human being on Earth. Her husband, too. They're the reason I'm here. So, if you don't mind, Elise here is going to join me for my song, and while mine won't be anywhere near as good as hers, I'm going to give it a try. So... You guys ready for some 90's cheese?"

One wiseguy in the crowd yells, "I'll listen to anything from you two!" It gets a few laughs. I wonder if that's the same son of a bitch that keeps booing me.

"So," Jamie says, "Archie, this one is from the both of us, just for you. Again."

The band starts playing and the crowd cheers and laughs, but not at my girls, at their song choice. It's the late-nineties cheese-fest from one of the many N'Sync and Backstreet Boys knockoffs, LFO.

Summer Girls.

It's one of my biggest guilty pleasures of all time. The song is absolutely atrocious by literally every standard. But god damn it, I love it.

The girls are taking turns singing the horribly asinine lyrics – Chinese food making someone sick, and Michael J. Fox being Alex P. Keaton - and the crowd loves it. Something tells me this place is filled with an awful lot of people around the age of forty.

It's incredible, and the most fun I've had in months. Maybe even years. I'm back on my feet.

When the night ends, we hang around out front for the band to come out, our ears still ringing, still high off the pure enjoyment of the night.

A lot of people on their way out stop and tell Elise and Jamie how well they did. One guy even took a selfie with them. Elise's smile is electric.

The band's bassist, a dude with curly black hair and a swagger that just oozes cool, steps out the front door, recognizes Elise, and makes his way over to us.

"Good show tonight, girls."

Elise jumps up and down a few times then wraps her arms around him. "You guys are so awesome!"

"I'm Ziggy. Real pleasure to meet ya'll."

"Same!"

We're making our introductions when the other two members of the band walk out and join us. The blonde drummer wearing the tallest heels I've ever seen seems a bit distracted, probably exhausted, and introduces herself as Monica.

"Hey," I say, "we have a Monica, too."

Our Monica extends her hand and they shake. Neither of them seem too amazed that they share a name.

Elise notices Other-Monica's heels and says, "I love your shoes! You don't drum in those things, do you?"

She laughs and says, "No way. I don't drum in them and I don't drive in them, but everything else, for sure."

"I would imagine driving might be a little difficult, too," Elise says, still beaming.

"Barefoot all the way, baby."

I stop myself from telling her I think it's illegal to drive barefoot but realize how stupid it sounds just in the nick of time. I think that's one of those urban legends, anyway.

The guitar player, another girl, this one much shorter, probably about five feet or so and with a dark ponytail, introduces herself as Mitzi. She tells Elise and Jamie that she had a blast tonight and hopes that we'll come back again.

"Absolutely," Elise says. "We don't live far."

"Great," Mitzi says. "We're off tomorrow and every Sunday, but we do live music Mondays and Tuesdays, and Thursday, Friday, Saturday. Nothing like tonight, just little background stuff for the guests. Live-band karaoke is every three weeks or so, usually with a different theme, which gives us enough time to get the catalog down."

"That's amazing," Jamie says.

"How did you know the NOFX song?" I ask.

"I'm a fan," Ziggy says. "I'm a fan of a lot of music. I started with playing calypso, then reggae, but I've always been a punk fan. The majority of the time here, I have to play generic beach-themed or top-forty bullshit. When karaoke rolls around, I want to add some stuff I like. You dig?"

"I dig. It was incredible."

"Hey wait," Ziggy says, "Archie Lemons... I know that name. And Elise Lemons. Holy shit. Ya'll had that movie..."

Elise nods. "Yeah. That was about us."

"Ya'll investigators or detectives, or whatever, right?"

"That's us," Elise chirps.

"That's sick!" Ziggy says, and then explains who we are to his bandmates, who both feign recognition.

I'm already embarrassed.

I prefer to remain unrecognized.

The kids are gathered around the car, making almost as much noise as the drunks made during the show. "I think we better go before the neighbors start to complain," I say.

"Hold on," Elise says, holding her phone. "I want a picture with the band." She holds her arm out, and Ziggy, Mitzi, and Other-Monica crowd in around her.

She snaps a few pictures, thanks them, then returns the phone to her purse.

"Thank you, guys!"

"Of course," Monica says, pulling her own phone from her purse and checking it.

"We'll totally be back," Jamie says, wrapping things up.

We say our goodbyes, pile into our cars, and head for home, the high from the night not wearing off any time soon.

ELiSE

"I was thinking," I say to Archie when we finally roll out of bed in the morning, "we should probably go to the local sheriff's office and introduce ourselves."

"Huh?" Archie says, not really awake yet. "Why would we do that?"

"Because, I mean, eventually we'll probably get back to work and it's not a bad idea to get in good with the local law enforcement."

"Aw man," Archie whines. "The local fuzz? Come on, we don't want to deal with them."

"Maybe it'll be different here. Maybe they'll be cool."

"And maybe I'll binge watch *Friends*. Get real."

"Oh stop. Come on, it won't be so bad. We can make a day out of it. We have a lot of exploring to do anyway. Come on, come on. Sunday Funday!"

"How about tomorrow? I promise. There's a Dodger game on today."

"There is literally a Dodger game on every single day until the end of October."

"I know. Tomorrow. Pretty please with sugar on top?"

"Okay," I say. "Monday Funday, then!"

Maybe sightseeing on a Sunday isn't such a good idea, anyway. You never know what fun places might be closed in these little towns.

"Monday Funday," Archie says, not matching my enthusiasm.

"Oh!" I say, remembering something. "The rocket launch is rescheduled for today anyway!"

"I'm down for that," Archie says. "Wait. This isn't one of those Elon Musk pieces of shit, is it?"

I laugh. "Of course not, babe."

"Hate that guy."

"I know you do, honey. It'll be okay."

"It'll be a cold day in hell before you see me in a Tesla!"

My husband has many arch-nemeses. His latest happens to be Elon Musk. Archie went off on his reasoning for this for about two hours a few months ago. Honestly, though, my memory retention of that specific rant is spotty at best. But I did hear enough to figure out that no matter what rocket or ship is being launched, to always say that *of course it isn't an Elon Musk one*. He refuses to watch the news unless it's forced upon him, so he'll never know the difference.

Not like it matters much. Archie's previous arch-nemesis was solar panels, so I don't hold too much stock in his grudges.

Plus, I'm in a great mood.

I have to admit, last night was pretty fantastic. And by pretty fantastic, I mean the best night, possibly, of my life. Taking the stage like that was a dream come true. That little girl from my past, with the abusive parents and no future, locked in that makeshift bedroom of her grandparents' house, doing ballet and singing along to Madonna, she would have been proud. I wish I could go back and tell that girl that everything would work out for her.

We invited the whole gang over again to watch round two of the launch. Everyone is in the backyard, eating the pizzas we ordered, and having a great time. The launch is on the TV so we can be ready. I have it muted in case anyone mentioned the words *Elon* or *Musk.*

The countdown is on.

3

2

1

It takes a few seconds for the sound to reach us, but when it does, it's incredible. A few more seconds later, the rocket comes into view above us, lighting up the late-afternoon sky with the extraordinary brilliance of a hundred fireworks. It's breathtaking.

The next morning, I almost have to drag Archie from the bed and throw him in the shower. He still manages to take a million years to get ready. When the bedroom door opens and Archie is finally dressed, I load the kids up in the car and we head out for the sheriff's office, which is only a few miles away. I know I told Archie that I thought it would be nice to introduce ourselves, which is partially true. I'd also like to inquire about any robberies where the perps got away with a substantial amount of cash and maybe, if there is time, ask about our bloated mobster.

I know the robbery probably didn't happen in Sunrise Cove, but maybe Cocoa Beach. These are pretty small towns. Perhaps the sheriff remembers a robbery like that in Palm Beach or maybe even Orlando. You never know, and it's totally worth a shot.

And, well... Honestly, I'm dying to find out whatever information I can about my old buddy Mongo. Something about that entire situation just screams *'More to this story!'*

The sheriff's office in Sunrise Cove looks more like a cabin. There is nothing about this place that screams law enforcement, but that's probably part of the small-town charm of little places like this.

"You guys mind staying in the car and watching Gary?"

"You got it!" Elliot yells from the middle row.

"Thanks, guys. Behave?"

Eric in the back, stretched out, too cool for school, says, "You know it."

We walk into the sheriff's office, a bell announcing our arrival. There isn't a soul in sight, so we walk up to the counter and take a look around. There are four desks behind the long wooden counter, that looks more like a bar top than anything else, each with a little table lamp on the edge, rolly chairs, and some files scattered about. Not much else. The walls are adorned with a few stuffed fish of some sort and various other plaques and photos of the area.

"Hello?" I call out.

A uniformed man of about sixty walks in from the other room, burping loudly before noticing us. "Oh, hi. Help ya?"

"My name is Elise Lemons. This is my husband, Archie. We just moved here less than a week ago. We're up in Bodfish Bay, the new neighborhood just up the street."

"Good to know ya. I'm Sheriff Murray. That's my first name, not my last name. Most people just call me Sheriff Murray."

"Well hi, Sheriff Murray. We stopped by for a couple of reasons. First, we're private investigators originally from California and then Montana..."

The cheer on Murray's face has vanished.

"No, no, it's nothing like that. We're just introducing ourselves. We've helped out on some cases before and we just wanted to, ya know, introduce ourselves, in case our paths ever cross."

"Well," Murray says, seemingly out of breath now for some reason, "that's fine, I guess."

"Where is everybody?"

"It's been a hell of a weekend, let me tell ya. You heard about the body that washed ashore? Fourteen hundred miles of shoreline in Florida and the sonofabitch has to wash up on my five."

"What happened to him?" I ask.

"He's gone. Back down to Palm Beach, where he belongs, finally. Thank the good Lord and good riddance."

"Palm Beach?" Archie says, suddenly joining the conversation after appearing to pay absolutely no attention before.

"Yeah," Murray says gruffly while stretching his arms out on the counter in front of us like he's bracing for impact. His jacket, which he is wearing for some unknown reason, falls open a little, and I see the very top of a flask sticking out of the inside pocket. "He's their problem now. He lived down there, or something. Hell, I don't know. I never heard of the sumbitch til he went missin'."

"Oh hey," I say, trying to change the subject and act like this is something totally off the top of my head. "Here's a random question for ya."

"Shoot."

"Within the past, let's say five years, do you recall ever having any robberies around here where they got away with a fairly large sum of cash?"

Archie shoots me a look. He's figured out the real reason I wanted to come. He rolls his eyes at me, and I can't help but smile.

"A robbery?" Murray says. "Nothing worth writing home about. At least not in this town. We get robberies here, but to call them successful would be laughable. Hell, two weeks ago, some jackass robbed an IHOP and stole plates of food and a chair and a server's table. Ran out in the middle of the goddamn highway, set up the table and chair and ate his breakfast with traffic whizzing by him. Semi got him, turned him into a pile of hamburger. So, any large cash robberies would be a hard no." He laughs.

"How about any neighboring cities? Cocoa? Palm Beach, even?"

"What's this all about?"

"This is just my own curiosity about something I read a while back."

"Hmm," Murray groans, obviously unsure if he believes me. "I can't think of anything. What kind of money are we talking about?"

"Oh, at least a hundred thousand."

Murray laughs. "No, not even close. You're new here, right?"

"Right."

"I'm sure you'll meet some of our criminals sooner

or later, and all your questions will be answered. I mean, maybe you can ask the sheriffs in Cocoa and Palm if they know anything, but I say no. Highly doubtful. Miami, maybe, sure. Anything is possible in Miami, but up here. No way. At least not without me knowing or at least catching wind of it."

I nod. "Fair enough. Maybe next time we're down in Palm, we'll pop in and see if they know. Like I said, it's not a big deal. Just my own female curiosity."

Men love that – *female curiosity*. They're so clueless about literally every aspect of the female mind that all you have to do is throw the word *female* in front of anything, and they'll buy it.

Men.

Archie is giving me a look again. He's hip to the whole scene.

We're about to say our goodbyes when the door chimes and in walks a man of about thirty-five, with disheveled hair, a dorky clean-cut full goatee and an untucked polo shirt. He looks like a stereotypical tourist that's had a bit of a rough night. His cologne scent follows him in and arrives like a punch in the gut.

Archie notices and winces.

"Can someone help me?" the man says.

"I'm the sheriff," Murray says. "How can I help ya?"

"My name's Chad Connors, I just got into town and I've already been robbed."

"Robbed how?" I ask, butting in.

Chad doesn't know who to look towards at first, then eventually decides on the sheriff. "My wallet. I had it getting off the plane, and now it's gone. I had to use an Uber to get here because I couldn't rent a car like I was planning on. At least I was able to pay for the Uber with my phone. Cost a small fortune, though."

"From MCO?" Murray asks.

MCO is the Orlando International Airport. It's jam-packed with tourists on their way to Disney World.

"No. The other one. Just out of town. Melbourne."

The smaller airport, closer to the coast. I've never

been there, and I've barely heard of it.

"Ah," Murray says. "Any idea where you think it was stolen?"

"As I said, I had it when I was getting off the plane. I know it. No doubt about it."

Florida is the Wild West, I swear to god. We've been here a weekend, and we have a briefcase of money, a tabletop hedgehog, a man fighting a flamingo, a bloated body on the shore, a rocket launch, an offer for some meth, and now some poor tourist getting robbed two seconds off the plane.

"We can fill out a police report," Murray says, "but honestly... I mean, unless someone finds it and turns it in, it's probably gone forever. Did you have any cash in it?"

"Of course I did."

Murray sighs. "Well, I mean, maybe it's best to just put a hold on your credit cards right now. I'm not saying give up hope, but... probably best to give up hope."

"Just like that? Nothing can be done?"

"What do you want us to do? You don't even know where it was stolen. I mean, there is a chance someone could find it and turn it in. We had a guy about two years ago hijack a car on A1A, then he realized there was a baby in the backseat. He looked at the registration, got the car owner's address, returned the baby to the poor parents, then drove off in their car and accidentally crashed it straight into a tree as he was waving goodbye. This is Florida. Anything can happen."

I'm trying not to laugh. Wild West!

"Shit," Chad says. "Is there a motel here that takes cash? I can pull some out at an ATM with my phone."

"Yeah, there are some places down by the beach that take cash. You don't have an ID, though, huh?"

Chad gives him a blank stare.

"Well, tell ya what, if the motel needs an ID, have 'em call me. Do you need a ride down to the coast?"

"No," Chad says, his mood already changing for the better. "I'll just walk. It's nice here, at least."

"Good luck," I say.

"Who the hell are you, lady?" Chad asks, annoyed with me for some reason and rather mean.

"We're nobody," Archie says in a matching tone. "Take it easy, *Chad.*"

Archie hates this guy so much. I love it. All it took was one snippy comment towards me, and Chad earned an enemy for life.

"Keep your wallet in the front pocket of those lame-ass khakis next time, *Chad.*"

"Yeah," Chad says before pushing the doors open and leaving, his lousy mood back with a vengeance, all thanks to my wonderful husband.

With Chad's back to us, Archie flips him off and makes a fart noise. "Take a shower, too!" Back to us, he says, "What the hell was that smell? It was like a fine mixture of dirty feet and a rotten fruit."

"It was patchouli," I say.

"That hippy shit?"

"Well, I think it was just a cologne with a patchouli scent to it. It wasn't real patchouli."

"How do you even know what patchouli smells like?"

I smile. "There was an old Madonna cassette tape that was patchouli-scented. Way back in the 80s. It was one of the only things I actually owned. That smell is imprinted in my brain for life."

"The tape smelled?"

I nod. "Yep."

"Why?"

I shrug.

"Which album?"

"Like a Prayer."

"That's a good one," Murray says, bouncing his eyebrows like he's Magnum P.I.

We talk to the sheriff for a few more minutes then take off. I really want to drive to Palm Beach.

—

62

ARCHiE

The shit-eating grin on Elise's face right now tells me all I need to know. She doesn't even have to ask.

"So," she says, about to ask me to drive to Palm Beach. "Let's go to Palm Beach. Whattaya say, kids?"

"Fish Tacos?!" Elliot yells.

"Yes, Elliot, I will buy you some fish tacos. Eric?"

Eric is looking down at his phone, his thumbs moving like lightning.

"Eric?" Elise says. "Tacos?"

"Yeah," Eric says, his thumbs never breaking stride. "Palm tacos."

Elise rolls her eyes at me, and I just shake my head. At least they're not having another farting contest, which is their typical car ride entertainment.

"Do you mind?" Elise asks me.

"Nah. It's cool."

"Wawa?!" Elliot yells.

Wawa is a minimart in Florida that we discovered on our first trip down here from Montana. It's enormous. The kids and I both love it so much, we refuse to get gas anywhere else.

"Yes," I say, "we can stop at Wawa."

"Hooray!" Elliot yells.

I pull forward through the Sherriff Station roundabout and make my way to the highway. The sun is blinding me. I'm not used to such brightness.

Elise notices and reaches into her purse and grabs a pair of Aviator sunglasses. "Wear these."

"It's okay. You can wear them."

"I have like four pair of sunglasses in here. No worries. Take em."

I put them on and instantly feel ridiculous.

The Palm Beach Sheriff's Office looks more official than our little Sunrise Cove office, which more resembles a take-out place for fish and chips. And to really drive home the point that we're in Florida, this one is located on Gun Club Dr., right between a state prison and the Trump Golf Club.

Yikes.

"You guys want to come in?" I ask the boys. "I don't give a shit about this place. You can tear it apart. Not like we live here."

Elise turns quickly to face me. Her stone-face gaze makes it seem like she doesn't want the boys in there with us.

"Um," I say, "maybe you guys should stay out here. But if one rich white guy in a shitty polo shirt with golf clubs slung over his shoulder approaches this car, you grab your little brother and run. You hear me?! You run!"

Elliot laughs, at least. I don't think Eric has realized the car has stopped moving.

"You're okay with Gary?" Elise asks.

"Yeah!" Elliot yells. "No sweat!"

Always yelling.

"Great," Elise says, opening her door and stepping out. "We won't be long."

"Then tacos?!"

Elise smiles. "And then tacos, yes."

"Score America!"

I have no idea what that means.

Elise closes the car door then takes a quick hit of her little pot pen thingie.

"Much better?" I ask.

She smiles. "Nerves of steal now."

Elise and I open the doors to the sheriff's office and step in, taking a look around. Much more official looking than our hometown office, we take a few steps towards the unmanned front desk and hope to get noticed.

A uniformed kid of about twenty notices us after a

few minutes and walks in our direction. "You guys been helped?" His nametag reads Martinez.

"No," Elise says. "We were hoping to speak with the sheriff."

"I think she's here. Might be a little busy, though. Beginning of the week and all that, and we had that... well, nevermind."

Elise smiles at him and says, "Think you could maybe go see?"

"It's important?" Martinez asks.

Elise dips her left shoulder and smiles again, "Sure."

The deputy smiles back and says, "Well, in that case."

I realize I'm still wearing these stupid sunglasses and quickly snatch them from my face and palm them.

"May I help you?"

The sheriff is a slender woman with honey brown skin that is so gorgeous it seems to sparkle. Her black hair is pulled into a ponytail so tight it smooths out her forehead. Her nametag reads Castillo.

Elise seems thrilled that the sheriff is a woman and quickly reaches out her hand to shake. The sheriff ignores it.

Elise side-eyes me briefly, then introduces us. "And we were just wondering if we could have a few brief moments of your time."

"Look, has a crime been committed?" Castillo asks flatly.

"No," Elise says, stuttering slightly. "I mean, yes, probably. But not to us."

"So how can I help you? Not sure if you noticed, but it's been a busy few days for us."

Elise chuckles. "The mob guy?"

Castillo mocks her chuckle and says, "Yeah, the mob guy."

"So how did he die?" Elise asks, going for it.

"Well, he fell off his boat and washed ashore, so obviously he hung himself."

Elise is quiet, unsure of what to say. She looks back and forth a few times as if she is searching for something. "Where's that deputy?"

"We're all busy. So, as impressed as we all are with you, we have big boy and girl work to do here. Maybe go snap a few pictures of my cheating husband or something and leave the real work to the pros."

"That's... not what we do... at all..." Elise trails off, still stung by the attitude she obviously was not expecting from her fellow female.

"Are we done here?" Castillo asks bluntly.

"Any major robberies in this area over the course of the past year or so?" I ask, matching her bluntness.

"Excuse me?"

"Robberies." I make finger guns and point them at her. "Bang bang, pew pew, money, hooray. A robbery?"

"How should I know?"

"Because you're the sheriff?"

"No, there haven't been any *major robberies* around here. Now if you'll-"

She's cut off by a very loud rustle of several people snapping to action around the office.

"What is it?" Castillo asks a rapidly approaching deputy.

"Uncle Sam struck again!"

"Where?" Castillo asks.

"Beachwood Park! Right in broad daylight again."

"Did he get away?"

The deputy shrugs and hustles past us. Castillo doesn't waste any time saying goodbye. She races back to her office, grabs a few things, then whizzes by us, leaving us all alone. Elise and I just stare at each other for a moment.

"Well, alright then."

We're about to leave when Deputy Martinez approaches.

Elise flashes him another smile and says, "What was that all about?"

Martinez breathes out a loud sigh. "Some guy in an

Uncle Sam mask just killed someone in Beachwood Park, which is only like a mile from here. This is his fourth one."

"His fourth killing?" I ask.

"Yeah."

"Hold on," Elise says. "Some guy in an Uncle Sam mask has killed four people and I haven't heard about it?"

"I mean," Martinez says, "yeah. It's like every two weeks. We have no idea who he is."

"Who are the victims?" I ask.

"Randoms as far as we can tell."

"Every two weeks and with randoms?" Elise clarifies. "That seems a little fishy. Right?"

Martinez shrugs, but she's right. There is nothing random about this.

"Look, I'm just telling you what I know. I'm sorry. I really have to go."

"Who was the victim this time?" Elise asks as Martinez is halfway out the door.

"Just some man. I don't know."

I snap my Aviators open and hold them in my fingers. "I guess," I say, with as much dramatic flair I can muster, channeling my inner-Caruso, "Uncle Sam wanted him... *dead*." I slide the shades back over my eyes.

Cue *The Who.*

Yeaaahhhhhhhhhh

Elise laughs so hard she has to bend over to help her breathe.

"Now come on, you know we have to follow those cars!"

ELiSE

Archie's stupid *CSI: Miami* joke was so perfect and so unexpected that I still can't stop giggling about it. We're literally following police to an active crime scene where a man was just murdered, and all I can think about is *Yeeeaaaahhhhhh.*

Maybe I shouldn't have taken that hit of Strawberry Cough before walking into a sheriff's office. Oh well. This is the Wild West. There are no rules.

Eric has actually put his phone down and is ready for some action. Elliot, too. Gary... well, Gary couldn't care less. He's just along for the ride.

"Right!" Eric yells, causing Archie to brake and make a sharp turn down the street, following Martinez's car.

"Where did they say it was?" Archie asks.

"I forgot. Beach something park."

"Doesn't matter. I'm stuck on this guy like a hippy's dingleberry!"

A few more turns, and we see the park up ahead. Several sheriffs' vehicles are parked in the lot, so we circle around, trying to seem totally nonchalant, then take a parking spot on the street about a block up.

"Everybody out," Archie yells. "We're not leaving you guys alone for this one."

"Sweet!" Elliot yells.

"Yes!" Eric says with the most excitement in his voice I've heard in months.

To Eric, I say, "Get the stroller, please." To Elliot, I say, "Get your brother. Be careful."

"On it!" Elliot yells in my face.

The boys get Gary into a small banana stroller and wheel him up to the sidewalk. A meter maid is headed towards us, tapping a stick to tires and leaving behind a white mark. She's gorgeous - thin and tan with long blonde hair pulled into a ponytail on the top of her head. I can't help but wonder where all the average-looking women work in this town.

She silently approaches us, a small little spring in her step. I nervously smile at her as she smacks our tire twice with her stick, making an X.

"Dude! We *literally* just pulled up," Archie says, so annoyed and completely unfazed by her looks.

"Yeah," the meter maid says with a bright smile. "And now you have one hour."

Archie clenches his fists and blows so much air out of his nose he looks like a bull getting ready to charge.

"Why an X?" Archie asks through clenched teeth.

"It's my own personal flare. Everyone else just does one tap and moves on. Not me. I put an X. More personal. That way, there is no confusion as to who did it."

"X marks the spot," I say with a nervous laugh, knowing full well my joke was awful.

"Of course," she says to me before turning her attention back to my husband. "This way, *sir*, whenever you see an X on your car, you'll know it was me."

She smiles and Archie is about to explode.

To diffuse the situation, I introduce ourselves properly, explain what we do, then ask, "Do you know what happened up there, Ms...?"

"Smith. Just call me Chrissy, though. Smith sounds so generic. And no. Obviously, I'm not in my vehicle right now, so I can't hear my scanner. Must be something, though. I heard the sirens. Us meter maids aren't very high on the totem pole when it comes to information."

"I think there was a shooting."

"Wouldn't surprise me," Chrissy says. "There have been a few around here lately. More than usual, actually."

Taking a chance, I mumble, "By a guy in an Uncle Sam mask?"

"Oh no kidding?" Chrissy says. "He struck around here a few weeks ago. Just up the block, actually, and around the corner. A guy just coming out of his office."

"Right up there?" I say, pointing down the street.

"Yeah. I forget the vic's name, but he was leaving work around 4:30. Some guy in an Uncle Sam mask comes up from behind, *pop pop*, two in his head, then disappears down an alley. Happened so fast, nobody knew what to do. It's on my route. If I was there, maybe I wouldn't still be stuck drawing on tourists' tires. Oh well, such is life."

"You were off that day?" I ask.

"No. I work every Monday through Friday, 7:30 to 5:30. I was on the clock, just not on the street. Darn, huh?"

"What day was it?"

Chrissy thinks for a minute. "What's today? Monday?

I nod.

"Not last Tuesday, but the Tuesday before. "Yeah. June 25th, I think the date was. I remember it being Tuesday because I got my hair done that evening."

"Great. And there were others? Killings, I mean."

"A few, yeah."

"Do you know anything about them?"

"Nah. Like I said, low on the totem pole. Maybe Sheriff Castillo can help if you're really interested. She's not the... Well, I mean, the internet is your friend, too. He was wearing a Hawaiian shirt, though. With an Uncle Sam mask. That's something you don't forget."

"Interesting," I say.

"Was it you?" Archie asks, seemingly out of the blue.

"Was what me?" Chrissy asks, confused.

"Are you Uncle Sam?"

Chrissy looks shocked. "Are you asking if I put on a cheap Halloween mask and murdered four men in cold blood?"

"Yes. Was it you? Come on. Just admit it?"

"Archie," I say, putting my hand on his chest. "Come on. That's ridiculous and you know it."

"Fine," Archie says, taking a step back. "Wishful thinking, I guess."

Awkward.

"Hey," I say, breaking the silence. "Here's a long shot. Did you ever catch wind about any sort of robbery within the past couple years?"

Chrissy was still giving Archie the evil eye, but eventually let it go. "I've only been here fifteen months, and there are robberies all the time here."

"I'm talking about a very successful one. Lots of cash. At least a hundred thousand, probably more."

Chrissy thinks for a moment then shakes her head. "Nothing is coming to mind. It happened in Palm Beach?"

I shrug. "I don't know where it happened, so I'm just asking around wherever I go."

"Low totem. Sorry."

"Thanks. We'll let you get back to work."

"You mentioned the shooting was on your route," Archie says, still pissed. "What exactly is your route?"

"This street, up and to the left where the shooting was, then left down Willow Pine, left on Palm, then back here."

"So basically a circle," I say.

"Yep."

Archie mumbles, "One of the circles of hell."

Chrissy ignores him. I do, too. "Well, if we find out anything, we'll let ya know," I say, trying to talk her out of giving us a spite ticket as soon as we turn the corner.

Chrissy smiles and says, "Like I said, Monday through Friday, 7:30 to 5:30. You'd be surprised how much this one area brings in just from parking tickets alone."

Archie laughs sarcastically, and rather snotty, and says, "Yeah."

Chrissy can still see how obviously annoyed Archie is with her. She fingers the wound by saying, "Tick-tock,

Mr. Lemons. Fifty-four minutes remaining."

Archie is bright red. "Ugh, I really want her to be guilty."

"C'mon!" Eric says impatiently. "Let's go!"

"Yeah," Archie says, trying to get over his annoyance by focusing on something else. "Walk casually. We're just here for a stroll or something, okay? Wink wink."

"Wink wink," Eric says, and takes off walking towards the park, pushing Gary in front of him.

At the park, there are people gathered with a few deputies on crowd control. We make our way towards the action and stop at the end of the pack.

To a teen girl, I say, "What's going on up there?"

"I think some dude got shot."

She's obviously no help. "Stay here," I tell my family, then try to squeeze my way closer to the front of the pact. This is the closest I've been to people in two years. Almost feels weird.

A man is next to me now, so I gently tap his shoulder and ask him if he knows what happened.

"Uncle Sam strikes again."

"Can you elaborate on that a little?" I say, smiling.

"A guy in an Uncle Sam mask and Hawaiian shirt is killing someone every two weeks leading up to a massive Fourth of July massacre."

"Hmm. How do you know that?"

"I mean, I guess I don't, but it makes sense, right?"

I think it over for a second. "Um, sure. Why not. Every two weeks?" Fourth of July is this week, though. This guy's math seems to be a little off, but I don't have the patience to argue.

"Yeah," he says. "This is the sixth week in a row. I mean, no. Fourth in a... Six weeks total, every other week. Don't count the first one as a week, and then two weeks, two weeks, then-"

"I got it. Every other week now for a total of six weeks. Do you follow the case at all?"

"Just what's on the news, but you can't believe

what's in the media anymore, ya know. I have a feeling it's going to explode after this one, though. Four is too big to not be something much bigger."

"No suspects?"

"As the news says, police are baffled."

"No connection between the victims?"

"All men, so far. But that's all I know."

"Locals?"

The man shrugs. "Not sure. I would assume so."

"Thank you for your help, sir."

"No prob. You wanna get a drink later and, as the kiddies say, Netflix and chill?"

"No thank you," I say as quickly as possible, already making my way back towards the fam, trying not to gag.

From the crowd, I hear the man say, "That means humpin'!"

I cringe and hope my kids didn't hear that. I quickly try to fill them in on what I've learned, which, unfortunately, isn't much.

"Now what?" Eric asks, seemingly deflated. "We can't leave. We have to solve this thing."

"Not that easy, kid," Archie says. "Not this time. Neither of us is licensed, and we are nobody here. Plus, this is a police matter."

"Not being licensed or it being a police matter has never stopped you before," Eric says truthfully. "Your moral compass is a little off-center," he laughs.

"It's barely off due north!"

"You broke into a guy's house to convince him he was being haunted by ghosts."

"That was no *guy*. That was that a-hole Hanley, and he deserved it."

"I'm just sayinnggggggg," my growing-up-too-fast son says, "the inconvenience of some laws hasn't stopped you from doing what you wanted."

To me, Archie says, "Kid's got a point."

"True," I say. "That gives me an idea. We can get an internet police scanner. Tune it in to Palm Beach and see what we can find out."

"Why?" Archie asks, dreading more work.

"Because I'm nosy."

"Is that legal?" Archie asks.

"It's not, not to my knowledge, not legal. I could be mistaken, though."

My boys laugh at the absurdity of my statement.

"Cool," Archie says unenthusiastically. "What are they going to do? Arrest us."

"I mean, yeah, maybe," I say, then laugh. "Don't act like a masked killer roaming the streets isn't exciting to you. You spend twelve hours a day watching masked killers slaughter people on your giant TV that hangs out into the hallway, so-"

"Those are movies. I'm safe when the killings are in moooovies."

"Oh stop. We're safe here, too. We're not going to hunt this guy down, but if we collect some facts, do a little digging... maybe we can help prevent more death. Isn't that what we want?"

Archie sighs, defeated. "I guess."

On the ride home, I find and download an internet scanner to monitor Palm Beach with from home. I'll download it to an iPad when we get back to Sunrise Cove and leave it on.

The more I think about it, the dumber my idea gets. It's not like we're going to be sitting in the kitchen, gathered around the iPad waiting for action.

So dumb.

I'll still do it.

But, so dumb.

Anyway, on top of doing that, I also found an article about our Mr. Mongo from the ocean. Turns out, he's been identified with a near-match DNA sample from his sister, who is locked up in New Jersey, and an identifying tattoo, and ring, just as suspected earlier. The DNA is the clincher, though.

This article is eighteen hours old.

I am way behind.

And it's amazing how fast law enforcement can work when it's something they really want. If we needed a DNA match test, we'd be lucky to get it by the next pandemic.

I guess the feds have a little more authority.

No news on the cause of death other than an accidental drowning. No signs of foul play, either. The only thing the medical examiner discovered was a non-fatal blow to the head, which happened minutes before drowning. It's the examiner's guess that Giuseppe was struck by something on the boat, or slipped and hit his head, before going overboard.

Shit.

Maybe I was wrong about this one.

ARCHiE

We managed to get the boys their fish tacos and beat the traffic on the way home, which means I can enjoy my evening Archie Style. Which is, ya know, eating and watching a crappy movie. I let Elliot pick tonight's since Eric got the last pick.

After scrolling around for what seemed like an hour, Elliot finally decides on *The Burning*, a summer camp slasher from 1981 starring a very young George Costanza himself, Jason Alexander. It's about a caretaker named Cropsy that was burnt severely during a prank gone horribly wrong and left for dead. Well, he's back now, and he's pissed.

The director, Tony Maylam, went on to direct about fifteen or so more movies, none of which you have seen unless you're a glutton for punishment or a die-hard Rutger Hauer fan.

Too bad, too, because this one is pretty good.

We're not twenty minutes into the movie when there is a knock on the door. This confuses me. None of the people who come here have ever knocked. Literally never. Poor Jamie has seen me shirtless more times than any woman should ever have to endure, yet she still walks right on in.

Another knock. Not sure where Elise is, so I guess I'm up. Elliot pauses the movie, and I do my old-man walk to the door.

When I open it, Ziggy and Mitzi from the karaoke band are there. I'm confused for two reasons. One, why are these strangers here, and two, how do they know where I live?

"Archie," Ziggy says, offering his fist for me to bump.

I do.

"What's up, guys?"

"You got a minute?" Mitzi asks.

"Yeah," I say. "For sure. Everything okay?"

"Not sure," Ziggy says.

"Hold on." To the boys in the other room, I say, "Hey, go get your mother for me, would ya?"

"Okay!" Elliot yells. I hear him run down the hall.

"You guys can come in."

Ziggy and Mitzi step into the house, and I show them to the kitchen. "You guys want to sit?"

"Sure," Ziggy says, pulling out two chairs for him and Mitzi.

"Hey guys!" Elise says before noticing their seemingly somber mood. "What's wrong?"

"It's Monica."

"Our Monica," Mitzi clarifies. "Not your Monica." She forces a smile.

"What's wrong with her?" Elise asks, taking a seat.

"We can't find her." Mitzi says.

"What do you mean?" I say, joining them at the table. "When did you see her last?"

"When we were all together. Saturday night."

"It's only Monday," I say. "And weren't you guys off yesterday anyway?"

"Yeah, but..." Ziggy says before trailing off.

"It's not just one day she's missing," Mitzi says. "It's three performances. We perform during breakfast, lunch, dinner, and late-night. We came here after the dinner show where we just did acoustics. If she's not there for late-night tonight, that's four performances she's missed. And I called her yesterday morning and she seemed distracted. Like, more so than normal. She's always been a little paranoid, but this was noticeable.

"So, you know what I did last night? I called her back. Just to see how she was doing, you know, be a good friend."

"And?"

"And nothing. Straight to voicemail. I betcha I called ten times. Straight to voicemail each time. I left a few messages the first couple of times, you know, then I just started hanging up. I didn't... I mean, I got kind of annoyed with her, you know. Like, why aren't you answering my calls... I was almost mad. But then, in the morning when she didn't show. Well, I knew something was wrong. I had this pit in my stomach."

"She doesn't normally miss performances?" I ask.

"Literally not one ever," Ziggy says.

"How long have you guys been playing together?" I ask.

"Almost four years."

"And she's never missed a performance?"

"I mean, maybe, but it was never just a no show. I mean, everyone gets sick and stuff, but no, never just not showing up."

"Yeah," I say. "I get that."

"Something isn't right. Like I said, missing a show is no big deal, but there is no way she would have left us hanging without letting us know, ya know?"

I'm fighting back the urge to ask how they found our address, but I resist it. The missing girl seems more critical at the moment.

"What time did you call her first yesterday when she didn't answer?" Elise says.

"Hold on," Mitzi says, "I can give you the exact time." She pulls out her phone, taps it a few times, then says, "4:08 pm." She then lists all the other times.

4:08 on a Sunday afternoon. We were still all in our backyard having a great time after that rocket launched, and Monica was missing. Hmmm.

"When did you first call her? When she answered?"

"10:12 am."

"So from 10:12 until 4:08, something happened that caused her to stop answering her phone."

"Not just stop answering it. It's like it was... when I said straight to voicemail, I meant, literally, straight to voicemail. No rings, no nothing."

"And you've tried calling today, obviously," Elise says.

—

"Of course. We even went to her apartment."

"No answer?"

"No answer," Mitzi says, "and her car is missing."

"What's her full name?" Elise asks.

"Monica Gargan. Not sure if she has a middle name or not."

"That will be enough. What kind of car does she have, do you know?"

"Range Rover. A black one."

"New or old?"

"Um, I really don't know."

"Probably about five years or so," Ziggy says. "It's not the newest design model, but it's the second newest. It's a sweet little ride."

"Can you give us her address and phone number?"

Mitzi nods. Elise grabs a paper and pen from the counter behind her and asks Mitzi to write it down.

"You think something happened to her?" Mitzi asks, sliding the paper back to Elise, uneasiness in her voice.

"I would try not to worry," Elise says, putting her hand on Mitzi's shoulder. "People take off all the time for no reason at all or every reason in the world. When they do, they usually return. Let me give you my number."

Mitzi pulls out her phone and programs Elise's number into the contacts app. "Got it."

"Great," Elise says. "Call us if she misses the late-night show tonight and the morning show tomorrow. I can go to the sheriff's office and ask a few questions. See if I can find out anything, but please *try* not to worry. I'm sure she is fine."

"I'm glad you're so sure," Mitzi says. "We're really sorry to bother you, but we knew if we went to the sheriff, he would have laughed us out of the office. You guys seem like the kind of people who would help. We can, ya know, pay you. I don't know what your rates are, but-"

"Don't worry about that right now. Just go back, do your show tonight, and try not to worry. If we do any work, you can pay us by getting Archie up on that karaoke stage some time and singing me a song."

Ziggy laughs, the first smile I've seen from him since knocking on my door. "You got it."

Fat chance, Zigmeister. Homey don't sing in front of crowds.

After showing Ziggy and Mitzi out, I turn to Elise and ask how the hell these people keep finding us. She ignores me. She's preoccupied with our Missing Monica.

For a couple of people who just moved to town, with absolutely no authority whatsoever, no private licenses, no offices, no ads, and no public phone number or address, we sure seem to have gotten quite busy, quite fast.

This is worse than that week when Elise tricked me into going back to our hometown for my high school reunion.

Although, that day turned out to be one of the best days of my life, so maybe my wife does know what she's talking about.

ELiSE

Morning has come, and with it, another missed drumming performance at The Gull. I'm not exactly sure what I should do. I've tracked down missing people in the past, but at least those times I was prepared and had services I could use to aid me. Here, I barely have unpacked suitcases and an internet connection. I have no real lay of the land, nor any useful contacts, aside from half-drunk Sheriff Murray and the less-than-chipper Sheriff Castillo.

I guess introducing myself to Murray was better than nothing. It wouldn't hurt for me to stop by later. Maybe right now I can drive out to Monica's place and see if she is there. Perhaps I can even sweet talk the landlord into opening her door for me.

Speaking of doors, ours opens, and in walks Milo.

"Hi!" he says to me with a wave.

"Hi, Milo! You want some updog?"

"Um. What's updog?"

"Nothin' much! What's up with you?"

If you've ever dropped raw meat on your kitchen tile, you'll recognize the thud my joke just made.

"Nothing," he says, oblivious to my updog remark.

"What's that you've got there?"

"Oh... I got a metal detector."

He holds it up with as little enthusiasm as possible, an almost frown on his face.

"Cool," I say. "Going to find some treasures?"

"My parents said that if we go down to the beach, sometimes people lose things and we can search for them." The way he is saying this makes me think he believes this to be some sort of punishment from his moms.

"Sounds fun."

"Maybe in like the 1800s. Besides, they said if we found anything valuable we'd have to turn it in, so I'm not really sure what the point of it is."

I'm sure the point is to get Milo out of the house for some peace and quiet during a seemingly endless time together in quarantine and now summer vacation. I don't say that, of course.

"Yeah, but if you turn it in and nobody claims it, it's yours."

"Yeah... I guess."

"It'll be fun. The boys are in the back."

Milo takes off running towards the backyard, his normal cheery mood returning as soon as he drops the metal detector behind the sofa with no regard for its safety, "K thanks!"

Since Milo is here, so much for me dumping the kids off at his moms', who apparently had their own plan. I can run out to the apartment alone. That's no big deal.

I walk to the bedroom, put on some jeans and shoes, and tell Archie and the boys I'll be right back.

"You need help?" Archie asks.

I smile. "Not yet. Later?"

"We'll be here. Be careful."

"Always."

In regards to my jeans, Archie says, "Those things are painted on. Don't get overheated. I think the weatherman said it could hit a thousand today."

"I'm fine," I say, kissing him on the top of his head. "Thanks for worrying."

"Always."

Back inside, I grab my keys and head out the front door to see Jamie standing there. We startle each other.

"Good god," she says, her hand over her heart. "I was just about to grab the doorknob.

I laugh and say, "You busy?"

"Nope."

"Go for a ride?"

"You know it!"

We get into my car and leave. I give Jamie the address and tell her to plug it into her maps. Siri tells us it's an eleven-minute drive with little-to-no traffic.

"Where are we going?"

"Monica, the blonde drummer from the other night."

"Yeah?"

I fill Jamie in on everything that's happened in the last twenty-four hours. She's in disbelief. "When we first met," she says, "did you ever dream you would lead this exciting of a life?"

"Honestly, James, I don't think I even thought I'd live this long."

"Oh, stop it right now."

"Seriously. But no. There is never a dull moment anymore. No complaints."

"Thanks for letting me tag along. I haven't done this with you in years."

"Of course. You can tag along whenever you want."

Jamie laughs and says, "Oh, don't say that, babe, you'll never get rid of me."

"Never want to."

Siri was almost spot on with her time estimate. We park in a guest spot and get out of the car. On the paper, Mitzi wrote down that Monica's apartment number was 125. I had no idea where it was. This wasn't an apartment building, more of a complex. Several two-story units are scattered around a manmade lake. Each unit houses maybe four apartments each, at least from what I can tell. Up ahead, there is a map of the property. We walk to it and find 125. It's on the lower floor.

This place is super cute. Monica has a little stream outside her front door and along the far side of the building, leading into the lake that should be on her back patio. It's an adorable apartment.

Jamie knocks on the door. Surprising exactly nobody, there is no answer. We walk around the unit, trying to peek into a window. All the shades are drawn, so we can't see squat. Just to be on the safe side, I walk back to the door and check the knob. You never know.

Locked.

Some jerky frat-boy type dudes are on their upstairs balcony a few units over catcalling us. They just invited us up for a drink.

We laugh it off and walk around the perimeter to find Monica's parking space. The frat-boys' catcalls aren't as friendly as they were a few seconds ago, now that we're leaving. In fact, they're downright disgusting.

Jamie takes hold of my hand and gives it a little squeeze. "It's okay."

Ah, such it is, being a woman.

They're still going even though we're totally out of sight now. We went from being *smokin' hot* to being *stuck-up whores*, among several other things, in the matter of seconds.

Jamie, still holding my hand as we're headed towards the parking lot, says, "Don't let it bother you, babe."

"How are we sluts if we obviously don't want to sleep with them?"

"Because they're idiots, babe. Literal idiots. Look at you. They're not even deserving of your presence anywhere near them."

I sigh. "I guess. But what gives them the right to speak to us like that?"

"Nothing gives them the right. They feel entitled to it. That's the problem. Those fools have a lot of un-learning to do if they're going to succeed these days. Believe me. We'll win." She squeezes my hand and starts swinging my arm as we walk, like children do. "We'll show them."

I smile at my beautiful blonde best friend and say, "Yeah, we'll show them."

She smiles back, bigger and brighter. "Come on, here's where it should be, right?"

Just like Mitzi and Ziggy said, Monica's car is definitely not here. There is only one black car in the whole row, and it's not a Range Rover. Not even close.

"Well," Jamie says, stumped.

"Let's go talk to the apartment manager."

We get back to my car and I notice the chalk X still on the tire. It's faded, but it's definitely still there and it makes me laugh. Archie was so pissed for no reason about that.

"What?" Jamie says, noticing my unintentional smirk.

"Nothing. You had to be there. If I tried to tell you, it wouldn't even be funny."

"Thanks for saving me the time then," Jamie says with a smile.

I'm almost about to clean the mark off with my shoe but I decide against it. It might be funny to leave it on and see if Archie notices.

We drive up to the front building. On the office door, a sign reads *Out to Lunch. Back at 1*.

Shit.

A total waste of time.

"Now what?" Jamie asks.

"I guess we go home. Sorry to drag you out here."

"Yeah, how dare you show me a good time. Oh, you know what you should do? Come back here tonight when it's dark and have Archie pick the lock."

"Archie can't pick locks."

Jamie starts laughing before I even finish my sentence. I can't keep a straight face, either.

"That's a good idea. He has no qualms about breaking and entering."

"You forget I've seen him in action before. Remember the locked door at the beach?"

"That seems like a million years ago."

Back home, Jamie and I fill Archie in on our failed trip and Jamie's plan for later tonight. Archie just shrugs and says, "Sure."

Not a care in the world for him about the moral questionability of breaking and entering.

He's the best.

"We need to go see Sheriff Murray right now, though," I tell Archie. "Do you mind coming with me?"

"Sure. Boys come?"

I nod. "That's fine."

"Hey!" Archie yells, "we're going to the sheriff's department. Who's comin' with?"

The two surefire ways to get the boys to listen is to offer food or adventure. Anything less than one of those two things, and you're lucky if they even acknowledge your existence when you tell them something.

Eric, Elliot, and Milo come running onto the porch. Even little Gary is stumbling behind them, although he's just following his brothers. He only cares about the food, not so much the adventure.

"James," Archie says, "you comin' too?"

"You have room?"

"Have you seen that thing your best friend drives? We've got plenty of room."

"Then sure! Thanks."

"No sweat. Milo, call one of your moms and make sure it's okay."

"K!" Milo says, already dialing.

Once he gets the go-ahead, we all walk to the car where Archie does, indeed, notice the chalk mark still on the tire. "Oh son of a bee! Did she use spray paint? What the hell?"

I laugh, then come up behind him and wrap my arm around his shoulder. With my foot, I easily brush the sad remains of the chalk from the tire. "All better."

"That woman has earned an enemy for life!"

Looks like Elon Musk may have been knocked down to second place.

ARCHiE

"Yo, Sheriff Murray," I call out from behind the counter. Jamie stayed in the car with the boys just to stay out of the way. However, I can't imagine a situation where a woman that looks like that would ever be a catalyst to any sort of anti-progress. Between her and Elise, I'm pretty sure they could sweet-talk their way out of a prison cell.

I take a sniff. "Holy crap, you can still smell that asshole's hippy dog-wash cologne. It's like cat piss or skunk spray. It just stays."

"Murray?" Elise says while leaning over the counter, ignoring me. "You back there?"

Murray appears from the same room as before. This time, however, his shoulder slams into the doorframe, causing a picture to fall off the wall and shatter. He ignores it completely. "Hey guys! What brings you in here?"

There isn't a single look of recognition on his face.

"We were, ya know, here earlier. Introduced ourselves..."

"Oh!" Murray says, "Of course. Sorry, I'm gettin' old."

That could be it. Definitely isn't anything to do with the flask I can see in his pocket and his dragon breath.

"We were just wondering if there had been any sort of incidents involving a slim blonde woman around forty years old but doesn't look it?"

"What do you mean?" Murray asks.

"Any... any deaths of someone fitting that description that's come through in the past forty-eight hours or so?"

Murray clicks his cheek with his tongue and says, "Nope. Sure hasn't. Someone you know?"

His breath wafts past me like a car's exhaust. It smells like an old lady's fart blowing through an open flame. It makes me long for the previous scent of patchouli.

"Kind of," I say, trying not to collapse. "We're just trying to find someone. Nothing for the sheriff's department to waste their time on. Any abandoned vehicles? Towed vehicles?"

"I... really don't know. What's this all about?"

"Nothing," I say. "Nevermind."

Murray's radio crackles to life. "Uh Skipper," a muffled voice on the speaker says.

Murray responds, talking into the radio pinned to his jacket. "Yeah?"

"We've got a car down here on the rocks. Looks like he drove off the road and plummeted."

"What kind of car?" Elise says. Murray ignores her, so she asks again, this time, less calmly.

"Ah, hold on there, Gene," Murray says, then looks at Elise. "What?"

"What kind of car is it?"

"Hey Gene?"

"Yeah Skip."

"What kind of car is it?"

"It's a Range Rover. Black."

Elise's face goes pale.

"Is there someone in it?!" Elise asks impatiently.

Murray relays the questions.

"Hold on... Yeah, Skip." Gene says on the radio. "A blonde woman."

Shit.

"Sit tight, Gene," Murray says. "I'll be right there."

Murray grabs his keys off his desk and stumbles past us.

"Shit!" Elise yells.

"Come on, we're following him."

Murray led us about two miles up the road, along the coastline towards the cove our little town is named after, although I doubt he noticed us since he couldn't even keep his car between the lines. At one point, he even hit the curb. How his wheel didn't explode on impact is anyone's guess. Now he keeps braking for no reason. His giant boat of a car is a symphony of brake-squeaks and engine-revs that has ended the lives of three poor squirrels in less than four minutes. I'd call the cops, but... well...

Elise and Jamie were freaking out, and honestly, I wasn't too happy about any of this either. The kids seem excited about it, but they at least recognize the seriousness of the situation and are choosing to keep it to themselves, aside from a few smirks I caught in the rearview mirror about Murray's horrible driving.

Murray parks his car about a hundred yards ahead of us on the side of the road, somehow managing to run over one last squirrel before killing the ignition. His front tire is actually up on the goddamn curb. I slow down and hang back. The street doesn't look very dangerous, and I see no sign of a black Range Rover or even an ambulance.

I throw it in park and open my door.

"Do you want us to stay here?" Jamie asks.

"Do you want to?" Elise asks back.

"I don't know if I'm ready for a dead body just yet."

"It's never a good time for a dead body," I say. "Do us a favor, guys; stay up here and keep a lookout."

"For what?!" Elliot yells.

"Anything," I say, just giving them a nothing job, so they don't feel left out. "Can't be too careful out here, kid!"

"We're on it!"

Elise and I follow Murray up the road a bit, keeping pace and trying not to be seen. I don't want to get thrown out of the accident scene before even seeing the accident.

The road we're on is a couple mile stretch of nothing. It's mainly just a peaceful coastal road that goes between Sunrise Cove and Cocoa Beach, for locals looking to avoid A1A, the major highway a quarter-mile inland. It's not particularly curvy or even dangerous. In fact, not only do you have to jump a curb, which Murray proved isn't as difficult as I would have thought, you have to cross about fifty yards of grass and palm trees before plunging off the side and onto the rocks below.

Murray finds some steps leading down to the water and takes them very slowly, his arms held out like he's walking the high wire at a circus. We wait until he is out of sight, then follow. At the steps, we see the Range Rover. It's almost straight up and down, crushed in the front, and wedged between several large rocks. Two deputies notice Murray coming and wave him over. Navigating in the sand is proving to be quite the challenge for him. I would laugh and wish for him to fall if we were here under different circumstances.

In the distance, ambulance sirens blare.

We take the uneven steps two at a time and reach the rocky sand. We're noticed, so I decide to play it cool. When Murray turns around and sees us, I say, "Thanks for letting us come, Murray."

He's too drunk to remember whether or not he told us we could come or not, so he plays it off by ignoring us completely. That works for us.

"Which one of you is Gene?" Elise asks.

A lanky kid of about nineteen with hair so blonde it's almost white raises his hand.

"How did you find the car, Gene?"

A clearly nervous Gene says, "A jogger called it in, Ma'am."

"Not the same jogger that discovered the mob guy a few miles down the road?" She chuckles, totally insincerely, but she's just trying to get us as close to the car as possible and pretend that she is totally where she is supposed to be.

"No ma'am. That was down on the beach. Like, way that way..."

"I know," Elise says, "I was just teasin'. So what do we have here? Mind if I take a look?"

———

90

Murray is distracted making a phone call and trying to stay vertical, so we use the opportunity to take several more steps towards the car.

"Um..." Gene says quietly. "Who are you, ma'am?"

Another winning smile. "I'm Elise Lemons. This is Archie. We're here with Sheriff Murray." She doesn't wait for him to answer, just walks right on by him to the car. She has to climb about six feet of rock before she sees into the driver's side window.

I can see her shoulders slump, and it tells me all I need to know.

Shit.

The sirens are blaring directly above us. Elise drops down just as the sirens end their wail.

"It's her," she says to me with tears in her eyes.

"Shit." I wrap my arms around my wife and pull her in tight.

Into my chest, Elise says, "She's... She's up against the front windshield. No seatbelt, otherwise the airbag would've... She could have been down here since Sunday. She's wearing a different shirt than she was on Saturday night. I mean, nobody is going to find her unless they're leaning over the edge of the cliff and looking down."

Sunday would be my guess, too, just from the phone call evidence. I don't point this out to Elise. She is obviously too stunned to think clearly.

Poor Monica. This sucks.

The paramedics are making their way down the access steps with their gear. They move past us and up to the car.

Miraculously, the Range Rover's driver's side door opens. They're cutting through the airbag, making it easier to get Monica out.

"Hey," the lead paramedic yells. "We've got a live one!"

Elise pulls herself from my grip and runs towards the rocks.

"What?!" she yells.

"This woman is still alive," the paramedic says. "Barely. And I have no idea how."

Elise turns towards me and throws her arms open in shock.

The lead paramedic jumps from the rocks and orders an immediate airlift. "We've got to get this woman out of here ASAP," he yells into his radio.

The other two paramedics begin unloading their gear, getting what they need to properly extract Monica from her mangled car.

Elise calls Jamie and fills her in on what's happening. Before she even ends the call, the swoosh of a helicopter drowns out all other noise. It's hovering above us as a stretcher is lowered down to the beach.

The paramedics slowly extract Monica and carry her down off the rocks to the stretcher.

Elise stops breathing and turns pale. Something is not right.

"Holy shit!" she says, just as Monica is secured. To the lead paramedic, she yells over the helicopter noise, "Did you put those shoes on her?!"

The paramedic shakes his head, "No ma'am. She was wearing them!"

Monica is wearing those tall heels that she said she wears all the time... unless she's drumming... or driving.

Barefoot driving only for me, baby.

"This wasn't an accident," Elise says to me as Monica is being lifted away. "Holy shit, Archie, this wasn't an accident!"

"If I had to guess," I say, "I would say you are right."

"Why?" Elise asks, crying again.

I shake my head. I have no idea. "Come on, let's get a closer look at the car while everyone is distracted."

We climb back up the hill of rocks to the car and peek inside.

"Much easier with the airbag cut out," Elise says.

I check the gearshift. It's in drive and not neutral, which would have been a dead giveaway. "So what do you think?"

"I think," Elise says, "that someone killed her, or at least tried to kill her, then put her in this car and shoved it off the cliff into the rocks to make it look like she fell asleep while driving or something. Now, why? I have no idea. But she couldn't drive in those shoes. No way. She even said it herself."

"That she did. She was about your height, without the shoes, I mean."

Elise nods.

"Check the position of the seat. Is that about where you would have it, or did someone taller or shorter drive it here and forget to put it back to the right position?"

Elise looks it over and decides that it looks about right. So much for the two most obvious things. Fingerprints on the keys and the seat lever could come in handy, but we'll have to convince Murray to do that.

"Wait," I say, leaning closer into the car. "What the... do you smell that?"

Elise leans in, takes a big whiff, then looks at me, confused. "Patchouli?"

ELiSE

A million questions are flooding my brain right now, none of which make any sense. Why would anyone want to hurt Monica? I mean, let's say someone came to her house and tried to kill her, then dragged her to her car and staged this whole scene. Would Monica have been wearing those high heels while she was at home? That doesn't seem very likely. It's possible, sure, but probable? Doubtful.

So, if I go off my instinct here, that means she was somewhere else, not at home, and was attacked by someone who didn't know she drove barefoot. Which could be anyone. The only reason we know is purely by dumb luck.

Other than that, all we know is that Monica went MIA between 10 AM and 4 PM Sunday, two days ago.

Now, if you add in the patchouli cologne smell that lingered in the car, the same smell from that Chad douche that got robbed on his way into town yesterday afternoon... Well, nothing makes sense.

I fill Jamie and the boys in on what happened and tell them that, as of right now, Monica is still alive, although she sure looked dead to me. Which means she probably looked dead to whoever staged this whole scene. This means... "She's not safe."

"No," Archie says, "she certainly is not."

"She needs someone posted outside of her hospital room."

A small crowd has gathered at the cliff, watching the action.

"Hey!" Elliot yells. "There's that nerd that pulled up to the police station."

"Huh?" Archie says. "What nerd that pulled up to the-"

He stops mid-sentence.

"What?" I ask.

Archie nods. In the crowd is Patchouli Cologne Chad.

"Holy shit, Arch. Holy shit!"

"We noticed him," Elliot says, "because he pushed on the door like three times to get it to open! It's a pull door!" Elliot is laughing like crazy. "You should have seen him! Hilarious."

"This makes no sense," Archie says.

"Do you think she was," Jamie says, lowering her voice, "ya know?"

"Hookin'?" Eric says casually.

"Yeah," Jamie says. "That."

"These days," I say, "it doesn't even have to be that. There are a million dating apps that can link you up with someone close in like two seconds... but the timeline doesn't fit. And Eric, never knock a woman for doing what she has to do to survive. Got it?"

"Yeah," Eric says. "I wasn't knockin', I swear."

"Okay. I'm not mad, just sayin'. Anyway, I think we need to go have a little talk with Chad, regardless." I open my door and am about to step out.

Archie reaches across the seat and puts his hand on my arm, "No, wait. Jamie, do you mind walking over there and joining the crowd. He doesn't know you. He would recognize us. Best to not tip our hand at all."

Jamie snaps her seatbelt undone and hops out of the car like it's on fire. "I can do that!"

I pull out my phone and tap Jamie's contact. "I'm calling you. Just hold your phone and leave it on the call. Don't be suspicious, just act like you're listening to someone talk. Go stand next to him and see if he still reeks of patchouli cologne or engages you in any way. If he leaves, we can follow him."

"If he leaves, and you need to leave me behind, just go. Don't risk losing him because you need to pick me up."

I nod, and Jamie takes off, walking toward the

crowd. "This is so exciting," she says into her phone.

We watch her walk along the edge, her long tan legs drawing the gaze of several of the nearby men. She's doing a good job of acting like an everyday nosy citizen without any real cares in the world. When she reaches the crowd, I hear her ask someone what happened.

I can make out the woman's answer - *Some car drove off the edge and down into the rocks.*

Jamie makes her way through the crowd again and stands right next to Chad. Into her phone, she says, "Oh babe, you know that thing we were talking about? Totally. Like, an overwhelming yes."

"Great," I say, "just play it cool. Don't say anything that you wouldn't say in a normal conversation about what is happening."

"Yeah, totally. Some girl drove her car off the side of the road and down into the ocean, I think. Sir, is that what happened?"

She's talking to Chad. He doesn't seem to respond, or if he did, it wasn't loud enough for me to hear.

People from a nearby park are running over to see all the action, or lack of action now, and I lose sight of Jamie and Chad.

"You still there, babe?" I say.

"Yeah totally, my friend has to leave, though."

"Shit."

Archie starts the car and shifts it in to drive.

"Which way is he going?" I ask.

"Shit," Jamie says, dropping the act, "the crowd has doubled."

"I know."

"Hold on. I think he got spooked by something. He split pretty fast."

I can hear Jamie making her way through the people. She makes it to the street, where I catch sight of her again. She's jumping up and down and pointing to a car headed in our direction. "That's him! That's him! Go! Don't worry about me!"

"Love you! Turn your ringer on!"

"Love you, too!"

I end the call as Archie flips an illegal U-turn over the center divider and pulls up behind Chad, keeping a safe distance but about as subtle as a Michael Bay movie.

My ringer is going off again and I don't recognize the number. Shit.

I tap to accept the call and put the phone to my ear. "Hello?"

"Mrs. Lemons?" a woman's voice says.

"Yes," I say as Archie busts a right turn so hard I almost drop my phone.

"This is Bernita Perez from the Cline Center. We spoke a few weeks ago."

"Oh!" I say excitedly. The Cline Center is who we contacted about Gary's early intervention. "How are you?"

The kids are in the back, shouting directions for Archie, who has decided to hang back as much as possible. One look in his rearview and Chad would instantly know he was being tailed.

Archie is playing it safe, wisely.

"Is... everything okay?" Bernita asks.

"Couldn't be better!"

"Great," she says while Archie gets stuck at a red light and drops a rather loud f-bomb. I cover the mic on my iPhone and mouth angrily, "*Cline Center!*"

"Oh shit," Archie says quietly. "Sorry."

"It's okay," I whisper, removing my hand from the bottom of my phone and putting it on his leg. "Is everything going okay?" I ask Bernita.

"Yes," she says, "I was hoping we could come by this next week and evaluate Gary. I wish it could be sooner, but it's a holiday week and you know how that goes."

I'm smiling so wide I must look like a lunatic. "Yes! That would be great. Thank you so much!"

"Would Monday the 9th at 10 AM be okay?"

"Yes, of course. We'll be there. I look forward to seeing you. Thank you so much!"

Archie is driving slowly down a side street where we lost Chad. He's so annoyed with himself for not running the red light, but everyone else in the car appreciates it. You can't solve any crimes when you're dead.

"There he is!" Archie shouts as I'm ending my call with Bernita Perez. We drove in almost a complete circle. We're back down by the water about half a mile from where we started. Chad's car is parked in a motel parking lot, one of those dives that probably accept cash that Murray was telling him about.

Archie hangs back as we watch Chad get out of his car and walk into room seven.

"What did she say?" Archie asks me.

"Next Monday at ten."

"Great! Hear that, buddy?" He's turned in his seat and looking at Gary. "Finally able to get you some help." He reaches his arm back and rubs Gary's shaggy hair.

What a relief. With the Cline Center on our side, we'll have access to the benefits the city offers for special needs kids. We looked into this heavily before deciding where to buy these houses because even back then, it was evident that Gary was going to need help.

"Now what?" Eric asks from the third row.

"Well," I say, "we need to go get Jamie first, then we'll decide where to go from there."

Archie flips another illegal U-turn and heads back to where this all began. Jamie is there waiting for us. When she sees us, she runs across the street and hops in the car. "Find him?"

"Yeah," I say. "We found him."

"Now what?"

"What are your feelings on beachside motels that accept cash payments?"

Jamie laughs. "Just like college."

I join in her laughter. Neither of us went to college. In fact, Archie only lasted a few weeks before dropping out, too, so don't ever let someone tell you the lack of a college degree will stop you from fulfilling your dreams.

"Do you mind doing a little stakeout?"

"Really?"

"Really. We need to drop the kids off somewhere and-"

"Aw, man!" Elliot yells.

"Yeah, come on!" Eric joins in.

"We have to drop Gary off, at least. There is no way he is coming."

"Eric, Elliot, Milo," Jamie says, "you come with me. Guys, drop us off, tell us what to do, go drop Gary off with Tabitha. We can handle a little ol' stakeout, right?"

All three boys yell *yeah* in unison.

"Milo," Archie says, "Maybe you should go home, too."

"Noooooo, come on. I won't tell my moms, I promise!"

Archie has a history of letting Milo tag along during things where no kid should be, especially someone else's kid who has trusted you with their safety, and he has felt the wrath of Liz and Monica for it.

That was a while ago, and obviously, things are fine now. But I understand his apprehension.

"Please, please, please," Milo begs. "Please!"

Archie thinks it over for a second, then eventually agrees. "But this is our secret. Got it?"

Milo smiles his adorable gap-toothed smile and says, "Got it!"

To Jamie, I say, "You're okay with this?"

"Totally!"

ARCHiE

I park on the road near the motel and ask Jamie to come with me. We cross the street and enter the office. Jamie rings the bell, and a massively-overweight clerk shuffles out slowly to greet us.

"Can we get a room?" I say impatiently.

"Sure."

"You accept cash?"

"It'll cost ya double."

"Eff that noise." I pull out my wallet and hand him a credit card.

"How many hours?" The clerk asks, looking me up and down. "One?"

He laughs at his own stupid joke.

"What kind of motel is this?" I ask.

"I'm just bustin' yer balls, son. But you will have to pay for the whole hour regardless of how long you're in there." More laughter. I look at Jamie, completely dumbfounded. Florida really is like another planet.

"Three days," Jamie says. "Just run the card and come on."

I mouth the words *three days* to Jamie, unsure why she picked that specific amount of time.

Jamie shrugs and says, "ya never know."

Quietly, I remind her of the holiday rates. She doesn't seem to care. In fact, she's almost laughing.

The dumbass clerk hands my card back to me, along with a key, and says, "Room 4."

I grab the key, and we take off, not saying another word. Behind us, I can hear the clerk's giant lasagna feet sliding slowly across the carpeted floor.

Back at the car, I tell Jamie and the boys, "All you need to do is keep an eye on room seven. I really want to take a look in there, so call us if you see this asshole leave. If you see someone else show up, call us. If you see literally anything happen in or around room seven, you call us. Under no circumstances are you to interact at any time. You are here strictly to observe. Sit by the window, look out, then call us if anything happens. Seriously. Promise me."

"Don't worry, Arch," Jamie says. "We got this. Come on, boys! We're up!"

The boys get out and join Jamie on the sidewalk. After a few cars pass, they all run across the street, walk through the parking lot, and into room four.

"They'll be fine," I say to a clearly nervous Elise.

"I know."

In the distance, several loud bangs make us both jump.

"Were those gunshots?!" Elise asks excitedly.

"Nope. Someone is getting an early start with the fireworks."

"Scared the shit out of me."

We end up taking Gary with us to the sheriff's department. We needed to make a quick stop here before anything else.

Murray greets us at the counter but talking to him is about as useless as talking to one of my idiot dogs. I'm surprised he hasn't tried to lick his crotch then barf on my shoe.

"Where is Gene?" Elise asks, clearly frustrated with the stumbling Murray.

Murray doesn't respond. He turns around silently and falls into his desk chair with a sigh so loud it reminds me of every dad ever after a big Thanksgiving dinner.

"God damn it," Elise says, very annoyed, her patience with Sheriff Murray coming to a screeching halt. "Gene?" she yells. "Are you here?"

The young Gene comes in from the backroom and greets us. Unlike Murray, he recognizes us.

"Gene, we need you to do us a favor. That girl you

pulled out of the car, she's not safe."

"The Jane Doe?"

"She's not a Jane Doe. Her name is Monica Gargan, and she is not safe! You need to post someone at her door as quickly as possible."

Gene, clearly confused, asks, "Not safe? Why?"

"We don't have time to get into the whole story, but that woman was not in an accident. That was staged. I'm willing to bet the person who did it is unaware that she is still alive. Well, maybe. He may have been tipped off when he saw the helicopter airlift her out."

"He?" Gene says, surprised. "You know who it is?"

"Well... Not yet. We have a suspect."

"Tell me, who is it?"

"Gene, I promise I will tell you everything after you get someone to guard her room. Please."

I just stand there looking pretty. I've learned to let Elise do the talking, especially when it requires talking a man in to doing something. She's much more convincing than my stumbly-bumbly-irritated ass.

"Gene," Elise says sternly. "I don't care if you go down there and sit, but somebody has to go."

Gene is still standing there, unable to make a decision. He turns to Murray, who is snoring at his desk, his belt unbuckled.

Elise is so frustrated she screams. "Get someone down there now, goddamn it! Wake that drunken idiot up if you have to, but get someone down there. If anything happens to that girl, it's on you."

An extremely frustrated Elise yells a few obscenities then heads for the door. I follow. On our way out, Gene says, "I'll get someone down there right away."

Elise stops and turns around, arms open, "Thank you."

After dropping a very sleepy Gary off with Tabitha, our next stop is Monica's apartment. It's dark enough for me to pick the lock without anybody noticing. At least I hope it is. If it's not safe, we can wait it out.

Before, when this plan was initially hatched, we were still searching for clues about where she could be. Now we'll be searching for any clues surrounding the events of her attempted murder. Neither option was pleasant, but this one is far worse.

Still no call from Jamie and the boys. I guess that's a good thing.

"Should we call Ziggy and Mitzi? I figure they probably still don't know. There wasn't any time for the press to get to the scene, and, well, neither of them strike me as fans of local news."

"Yeah," I say. "Let's check Monica's apartment first, see what we can see. Then we can go from there. There's nothing they can do right now that would be helpful."

Elise nods her head. "Okay."

We pull into her complex, and I park in visitor parking. We get out of the car looking as carefree as possible, just a couple of people visiting a friend.

More fireworks in the distance. Can't these savages wait a few more nights?

At Monica's door, I slip my pick into the lock and twist. It takes me all of three seconds to get the door open, but when I do, it's quite the shocker. Her apartment has been completely ransacked.

"Oh my god," Elise says with a look of disgust on her face. "What the hell is going on here?"

"The mystery deepens."

"Hurry, close the door."

"Hello," I call out, just in case. Nothing.

The sofa is overturned, the cushions and lining ripped to shreds. The drawers are pulled out and emptied onto the floor along with all the food from the fridge. The few picture frames Monica had hanging up around the place are broken, the pictures removed.

"Well," I say, "someone was looking for something."

"Obviously," Elise says, "but the question is, did they find it?"

"I don't think so," I say, pointing to a hole in the drywall next to the door we just came through.

"Why not?"

"Looks like he punched a hole in the wall when he was leaving. That's not something someone does after a successful mission. He was pissed."

"Which means whatever he wanted isn't here."

"Or it is, and he just didn't find it."

I begin walking around the room, sniffing the air for any scent of patchouli. No dice. Oh well, worth a shot.

Elise is looking around, shaking her head. "I have no idea what to do."

"Yeah, this is a head-scratcher for sure."

"Do you think this place was torn apart before or after someone drove Monica's car off the cliff?"

I think it over and come up with nothing. "I really have no idea. It's possible this is what drove her out of the house in the first place. Or, it's also possible that she was attacked just to get her out of the way. It would make searching this place a lot easier. I really don't know."

"Well, shit," Elise says.

I put my arm around her waist and pull her close. She rests her head on my shoulder. "Well shit, indeed."

ERiC

I opened the curtains in the room and put my chair right by the door, just like Jimmy Stewart in *Rear Window,* minus the gigantic camera. This gave me the best view of anyone coming or going from room seven. It's been over an hour and nothing has happened. No one has even pulled into the parking lot since we got here, and the only noise is from fireworks off in the distance.

Stakeout work isn't very exciting. Richard Dreyfuss and Emilio Estevez lied to me, man.

Milo is swimming the channels with the TV on mute, Elliot is flat on his back on the carpet, and Jamie is sitting on the chair against the far wall, her legs crossed.

I love you.

God, snap out of it, Eric. Focus, focus, focus.

I look back out the window. Still no action.

I'm about to let Elliot take over the spying duties when some headlights pull into the parking lot, flashing across our room, lighting it up for a brief moment before pulling into a spot next to our dude's car.

A burly man with a shaved head and no neck steps out and moves to the trunk, where he grabs a paper bag filled with what I assume to be groceries or snacks.

He is literally chugging Diet Coke from a two-liter bottle.

He caps the bottle up and tosses it into his car through the driver's side window, belches so loud it almost rattles our windows, then walks to room seven and knocks. I jump to my feet, and everyone joins me at the window, all looking out.

"Holy crap!" Elliot yells. "Who is that?"

I shake my head.

"But who is he?" Elliot asks again.

"I don't know! God."

"He's a big one," Milo says, his face smashed against the glass.

"Get back," Jamie says, "get back. He might notice three kids with their faces pressed against the glass."

"You're right," I say, "everyone get down and stay out of sight. Just peek."

The door to room seven opens. The big bald dude stands there for a few seconds, probably talking to our guy, then walks inside.

"But who is he?" Elliot asks again. I want to smack him.

"I. Don't. Know." I say slowly. "But we better call Mom and Dad!"

ELiSE

"It's Eric," I tell Archie when my phone begins ringing. "Hey honey, everything okay?"

"Not sure. Some big bald dude just knocked on his door. He walked in holding a grocery bag. Snacks or something."

"What happened?"

"It kinda looked like they talked for a few seconds, then our guy let him in."

"Nothing since?" I ask, quickly telling Archie what happened in between my questions before deciding to just put it on speakerphone.

"No," my son says, "just a whole lot of nothing. Someone is setting off fireworks, but that's it. There's seriously been no one here except the bald guy since you guys dropped us off. Wait. Bald Guy is leaving. He's still carrying the grocery bag. This fool is so big he was drinking diet coke from a two-liter bottle, Mom."

"That sounds... weird," I say. "All of it. You guys don't move. Just stay in your room and stay safe. We'll be back over there soon. Call us if Chad leaves."

"Who's Chad?" Eric asks.

"Chad," I say, realizing I may never have told them who they were watching. "The guy we followed, sorry. The guy you're watching."

"Okay, we're on it."

"Everyone okay?"

"We're fine, Mom. Do what you gotta do. We've got eyes on this guy. No sweat."

I tell him I love him, embarrassing him to no end, I'm sure, then end the call.

"You know," I say to Archie, "we don't *actually* know this guy had anything to do with, well, anything. You said it yourself. The timeline doesn't work out."

"I know, he's just a suspect, but as for now, he's all we've got unless we find something here."

"We need to learn more about Monica. We really should meet up with Ziggy and Mitzi."

We enter The Gull and take a seat in the back, where we were for karaoke. The place isn't nearly as crowded, but Ziggy and Mitzi are on stage, doing some acoustic songs. It's terrific. The people here seem to be enjoying them as they eat and drink, but nothing like before.

Ziggy spots us and tells the crowd the band is going to take a little break. A minute later, he and Mitzi are sitting at our table. Archie and I break the news to them.

When they regain their composure, I get into the other reason we're here. "What can you tell me about her?"

"Like what?" Mitzi says. "We played with her, but she was a very private person. I don't know how much help we'll be."

"Well," I say, "did she date a lot? Did she have a boyfriend?"

"I never saw a guy in here with her, and we're here a lot. I don't imagine she would have much time for dating... at least without us knowing. I know I sure don't."

Ziggy shakes his head and says, "Me either."

"Okay," I say, moving on, "did you ever notice her on her phone a lot? Any dating apps that maybe she used during her downtime around here?"

They both shake their heads no.

Archie takes over. "Anything weird about her? Anything at all."

Mitzi says, "She was private like I said, but that's not necessarily weird."

"She seemed kinda distracted the night we were all hanging out in the parking lot. Was she like that a lot?"

"Every now and then. Sometimes it seemed like she would be looking over her shoulder. Not literally, but you know what I mean."

I ask, "Do you think she could have been running from an abusive relationship? I've been in one of those. I know what they can do to a person."

"It's possible," Ziggy says. "I mean, she never mentioned it. I would'a beat the guy's ass, ya know. I suppose it does make sense, though."

Chad didn't exactly look like the type of guy Monica would go for, but that doesn't mean anything. Did Monica escape from a relationship and hide. Was it Chad? And if so, did Chad fly into town and... Something dawns on me.

To Archie, I say, "If Chad had his wallet stolen, how did he get a car?"

"I was thinking about that earlier," Archie says, "when Elliot spotted him in the crowd. Elliot said, 'there's that dork that pulled up to the sheriff's office,' or something like that. I meant to ask him about it but got sidetracked by everything."

"Excuse me," I say to Ziggy and Mitzi as I pull out my phone. "Just give me one second."

"Sure," Ziggy says, sighing deeply, obviously worried about his friend.

I dial Eric's number. He answers right away.

I say, "Hi Honey Bunny Sugar Muffins, let me talk to Elliot real quick."

Eric says, "Ew, Mom."

A few seconds later, Elliot comes on the line. He's so loud that I have to hold the phone away from my ear. "Hi, Mom!"

"Elliot, honey, earlier when you spotted that guy in the crowd, you said he pulled up to the sheriff's office. What did you mean by that?"

"What do you mean?!"

So very loud.

"Like, did he walk or drive, or take a taxi... how did he get there?"

"Oh! He drove. He parked down by the street instead of way up by us then walked."

Archie hears despite my phone *not* being on speaker.

"Ask him why he even noticed this one random guy," Archie says. I relay the question.

"I didn't notice him until he started pushing on the door that was a pull," Elliot says. "When he left, I watched him walk down to the street and get in his car. Why?"

"I'll tell you later. You're absolutely, positively, sure that he was driving?"

"Yep!"

"Thank you! Get back to your stakeout and call me if anything happens, okay?"

"Okay!"

We say our goodbyes, Elliot not being too cool to tell his old mom he loves her, and then I hang up the phone.

To Archie, I say, "If Chad had a car, then his whole story could be bullshit. There isn't a car rental place on the planet that would rent to someone with no credit card and no license."

But why?

What purpose does it serve to lie about being pickpocketed at the airport?

Our guests at the table are even more confused than we are. I apologize and ask one more question. "How did you first meet Monica?"

"She came in here," Ziggy said. "We had been playing these acoustic shows for about six months before she showed up. She said she knew how to drum and asked if we were interested in expanding the band. Best decision we ever made, professionally at least. Better music means better tips, too, so it was a no-brainer."

"Did she say anything else?"

"I don't think so," Mitzi says. "She was very nice, maybe a little timid at first, but nothing weird. Oh, she did tell me I had nice veins. I thought that was very sweet. I mean, I have no idea what she meant but I took it as a compliment."

———

110

"Nice veins?" Archie says. "Sounds like something a vampire would say."

Mitzi laughs, "Yeah, a little."

"She isn't a vampire, is she?"

Mitzi laughs again and says no. When the brief moment of levity ends, the pain comes back with a vengeance.

Everyone is stone silent now. Ziggy's shoulders slump. Mitzi rubs her eyes.

It's weird when that happens. When one little comment can lift the weight of something enormous, but only for a few fleeting seconds before the cruel sting of reality comes crashing back down.

"When she came in, did she mention where she came from?"

"No, but she did mention Palm Beach a few times, real casual-like. It seemed like maybe she was from around there. Close, but not too close."

I reach out and grab her hand, taking it in mine. "Thank you guys so much for your help. We'll be sticking with this until we find out who did this to her. In the meantime, try to think of anything that could be helpful."

"And don't hesitate to call," Archie says, contradicting his ordinary motto of *Please* do *hesitate to call.*

"We will," Ziggy says. " I just don't understand why this happened."

"Us either, buddy," Archie says, getting to his feet. "But we're sure as shit going to find out, I can promise you that."

"I appreciate that."

"For sure."

Cutting through the Gull's parking lot, Archie says, "Even if Chad lied, we have no way of proving it. We can't pull airline records to prove he was on a flight, and something tells me ol' Drunk Murray, who is proving to be more and more worthless, isn't going to be Charlie

Hustle on that."

It's scorching out here. It's so hot that the asphalt of the parking lot is blurry from steam rising off of it.

Certainly, something you would never see in the frigid and boring confines of backwoods Montana.

I'm certainly not complaining. Don't get me wrong. I'm wearing the bare minimum of clothes right now and I absolutely love it.

The humidity makes me feel like I'm wrapped in a wool blanket, though.

Not complaining... Just sayin'.

Archie reaches into his pocket and pulls out those ridiculous CSI glasses I gave him. I can't believe he still has them.

He giggles when he puts them on.

Returning to the car, I ask, "So, what do we do?"

"I'm sure we'll figure something out."

We're just about to leave when my phone rings. "It's Eric," I tell Archie while answering the call. "Hi honey."

"Mom, he just got in his car and backed out."

"We're on our way."

ARCHiE

It only takes us ten minutes to get to the motel. In the parking lot, two shirtless guys are pounding on some fireworks with a hammer and laughing like a couple of drunken hillbillies. God knows why. We drive past them and park in front of room four. Eric comes out to greet us and tell us Chad is still gone.

"What do you want to do?" Elise asks me as we close the door to room four behind us.

There are an awful lot of face prints on the front window here that make me think this ace-squad of master stakeouters weren't quite as subtle as they could have been.

I think the plan over for a minute before deciding. "I want to take a look in that room. You never know. We could find something that proves we were totally wrong or totally right. Or we could find jack-shit. But we have the opportunity now so we should take it.

"Eric and Milo, can you go to that end of the parking lot and keep a lookout? Elliot and Jamie, can you stand by the other end? If he comes back, we won't have much time, so as soon as you see a car on the street comin' this way that could be his, you tell us."

To Elise, I ask, "Are three-way calls still a thing? Like, can we all be on the same call at the same time, or did that go out with velvet scrunchies?"

"Actually," Elise says, "scrunchies are coming back, but I have no idea about the three-way calls. At least not on a cellphone. I'm sure you can. Seems like a weird feature not to have for a phone that can literally tell you how fast your heart is beating."

"But you don't know how?'

"Not a clue?"

"Jamie?"

"Nada."

"Boys?"

"Making phone calls went out with the dinosaurs," Elliot says. "Gawd."

"That was my joke... You just changed scrunchies to dinosaurs."

"No, I didn't."

Sigh.

"Okay," I say, "forget it. Just have your phones opened to a text message to us. As soon as you see any car resembling his, you hit send, don't type anything... just send *anything*. Make sense? The farther out the car is, the better for us. You ready?"

Nods from the gallery.

I open the door, and we all step out into the blazing hot evening air. The shirtless idiots are running across the lot as a loud explosion destroys the motel's mailbox, sending shards of wood and metal into the air.

The shirtless idiots fall over laughing.

Elliot yells, "Yeah! That was awesome!"

The boys all share high-fives while the shirtless idiots take a bow.

"Good god," Elise says. "What is happening here? Florida truly is somethin' else."

The motel manager didn't even bother to waddle out and see what the ruckus was, and the shirtless idiots are already back to making another homemade cherry bomb.

"Stay clear of these morons, please," I say to everyone. "And stay alert."

Eric and Milo take their post to the south; Jamie and Elliot give us a thumbs-up from the north. I pull out my pick, and we're in room seven in less than ten seconds.

We close the door behind us quickly and flip on the light.

The room is almost identical to ours. One noticeable difference is the suitcase on the floor, and the art portfolio spread out on the bed, several drawings, pencils and pens, scattered all over.

He had none of this with him when he stumbled into the sheriff's office, and I'm irritated with myself for not realizing his lack of luggage at the time.

"What does this even mean?" Elise asks.

I shake my head. "I'm stumped."

Nothing makes much sense. I'm not even entirely sure this guy had anything to do with Monica. The apartment smells like the horrible cologne and the car, but that could be just a coincidence, I suppose. Her apartment didn't smell like it.

I just don't know.

Something crashes in the bathroom, startling us both and freezing us where we stand. My first thought is the shirtless idiots, but that can't be it. I can hear them out front hammering away.

Now there is grunting.

Elise and I run to the bathroom, open the door, and see Chad trying to squeeze his way through the tiny window while holding a bag of Burger King. With his ass and legs dangling outside, he yells, "Aw man, c'mon! Who the hell are you? Do you work for him, too?"

"You don't recognize us?" Elise says, wide-eyed and completely confused, trying her best not to laugh.

"Are you gonna kill me?" Chad asks, falling to the floor. His face was bloodied beforehand, but now it's just worse. He's taken a beating recently. To make matters worse, he just dropped his Burger King bag into the toilet. "Aw man, my burgers."

He pulls the bag out of the toilet. This causes me to take a step back. If he eats that burger, I am going to freak out!

"Why would we kill you?" Elise asks.

"Because, man. I messed up. I know I messed up, man, and you know it. But, listen, I can make it better." He's stumbling to his feet, fresh blood is leaking from his nose like a faucet, his hand still gripping the toilet Burger King.

Everything about this is repulsive.

"What did you mess up, Chad?"

"Who's Chad?"

Good lord. "You said your name was Chad. When we met."

"We met?"

Gawd!

"Yes. At the sheriff's office. You came in and said you got pickpocketed at the airport. We can't help but wonder why you would lie about that."

"We also can't help but wonder," Elise says, "why you are trying to squeeze in through the bathroom window when... there is clearly a door?"

"I... I hid the car, man... I wanted you to think I was gone. That's why I came back in this way. In case you guys were watching."

"I think you have us mixed up with someone else. Why don't we go into the living room and figure this whole thing out."

Chad, or whatever his name is, nods his head. "You're not gonna shoot me in the back, are you?"

I wink to Elise and say, "Not if you tell us what we want to know."

"Come on, you cowards. You wouldn't shoot a guy with an empty stomach, would ya?"

"Take a seat," Elise says, pointing to the table and chair by the window. He does as he's told, albeit rather slowly.

"Now, there is one thing we need to know," I say sternly. "And you better not lie to us."

Chad looks like he's about to pee himself. He nods and stutters out an, "Okay."

"You understand?!"

Chad nods his head nervously. "Yeah. Yeah, sure. I understand."

"Why," I say, my finger pointed directly at him, "do you smell so bad?!"

Elise facepalms herself.

"I- I smell bad?" Chad asks, sniffing his armpits.

"Awful! Infuriatingly awful!"

"I'm... I'm wearing cologne," he says quietly, now obviously more worried about his scent than being killed.

"Well, it's awful! You should sue."

"But..."

Elise takes over. "How about you start by telling us your real name?"

"Do... Do you mind if I eat my food?"

"If you want to eat your turd burgers, be my guest."

To Elise, I whisper, "Come on, no, please god, no."

She just shrugs.

"So," she says, "your name."

"Antonio."

"And your last name?"

"Russo. Antonio Russo. Tony?"

"Why Chad?"

Antonio shrugs.

"And why the ruse?"

"The what?"

"Why did you come into the sheriff's office and lie. We're just trying to figure things out here, so why don't you start from the beginning."

"You'll kill me."

I say, "We'll kill you if you don't tell us, that's for sure." I like this tough guy routine. "Although, I might die first if I'm trapped with this scent much longer.

"Look, I promise. I was... I think it smells good, man."

Elise sighs. "Stay on target, Antonio."

"Right," he says. "Sorry. I was... I was sent here to get something."

"What?"

"An envelope."

Antonio removes his burgers from the wet toilet bag and unwraps one slowly, his eyes never leaving Elise's.

"You were sent here to find an envelope, and that required you to lie to the sheriff? Let me change my line of questioning. The girl in the car in the rocks today... You saw her, yes?"

Antonio nods, his eyes still locked on Elise. He slowly opens his mouth and takes a bite of his soggy burger. It sounds like he's biting into a wet sponge and I'm trying not to throw up.

The look on his face is pure regret.

I almost feel bad for the guy.

Elise, handling this much better than I am, follows up her last question. "Well? Do you know who she is?"

"No," Antonio says, swallowing down his one, and only, bite of his burger. He wraps the rest of it back up and returns it to its bag. "I don't think I want these burgers, anymore."

Ignoring him, Elise says, "You said you messed up. What did you mean?"

"I messed up everything. It was supposed to go smoothly but literally nothing worked out right. I've never... I've never been in charge of anything before. I had a plan... a foolproof plan... but..." He shrugs and says, "Oopsie-daisy."

"Quit farting around and just answer the goddamn questions," I say, losing all patience with this idiot.

"I don't..." Antonio says, trailing off. "I don't think you're who I think you are."

This guy is sharp.

"My boss," Antonio says, "said he needed me to come down here and pick up some paperwork. That's all I'm doing."

"And who gave you the beating?"

"I fell. In the bathroom, remember? You saw it."

"Yeah, nice try. You remember we saw your face before you fell, right?"

"No, you didn't."

This guy getting a beating is starting to make more and more sense the longer he talks.

"And who is the bald, burly guy?"

"Pizza delivery man."

Shit.

"Look," Antonio says, "I just got to town yesterday. I'm going to get what I came for and go home. No big deal."

Elise picks up one of the drawings from the bed. "You an artist?"

"I've been drawing since I was a kid. I'm not great, but it's fine. I do tattoos, too. So if either of you wants one, you know where to come."

"I'm good," I say, fighting back every urge I have to just slap this guy.

"I mean," he says, "I've only done one but you've gotta start somewhere, right?"

I sigh, trying to subside my anger with this rambling douche.

I take another deep breath and ask, "Where'd you get this big portfolio? You certainly didn't have it when you came into the sheriff's office."

Antonio shrugs. "I brought it. *Bought it. Bought it.* Not *brought* it. Ha. Bought it." He's stumbling over his words like Clark Griswald talking to the underwear saleswoman in *Christmas Vacation.*

"Antonio," Elise says, "I have a sneaking suspicion that you've been in town since Sunday."

Antonio shakes his head nervously. "Nah. You're crazy. Monday Monday Monday!" He chuckles. Looking at me, he says, "Remember those old commercials for Monster Truck Rallies? Sunday Sunday Sunday!"

When neither of us responds, he clarifies, "But, in this case... Monday... Monday Monday. Just another manic Monday. Ha, you remember that song? Walk like an Egyptian..."

We're both glaring at him.

His shoulders slump and he mumbles, "Sorry."

Elise is so annoyed. She's scratching her palms; a surefire sign that someone has screwed up, or missed the toilet, again. "You went into that sheriff's office to establish an alibi. If you arrived on Monday and got pickpocketed, then anything that happened here on Sunday couldn't possibly have anything to do with you, right?"

"You're crazy. I got here on Monday. Monday.

———

119

Yesterday Monday. Not Sunday. Weren't you paying attention? You're crazy."

Elise holds up the drawing and shows it to Antonio. "What's this drawing of?"

"I don't know."

"You don't know? I mean, it's not exactly a masterpiece, but it's clearly a rocket."

"Yeah, maybe. I forgot. So what?"

Elise walks to the window and points north. "That's Cape Canaveral. Right over there. This rocket that you drew launched from there on Sunday afternoon." Elise holds the drawing up for all to see. Sure enough, the drawing matches the exact view from where Antonio is currently sitting, even down to the edge of the motel and the cell tower just beyond. "You were here on Sunday, Antonio, and I need to know why."

ELiSE

Antonio is just sitting there, completely still, dumbfounded. We nailed him, and he knows it. He hangs his head, resting it in the palms of his hands. "They were supposed to find her on Sunday. She refused to tell me where the envelope was, so I had to get rid of her so's I could find it."

"Who?" I ask, but I already know the answer. I want him to say it.

"The blonde down on the beach."

Anger swells up inside me. I want to unleash it on this moron so goddamn badly, but... Archie places his hand on my shoulder, trying to calm me down.

Someone was supposed to find her on Sunday, but they didn't. By Monday afternoon, I had already established my alibi, but... the car was still down on the beach. I couldn't believe it, I thought for sure."

"Why did you dump it on a beach," Archie asks, "that's so well hidden if you wanted her to be found right away?"

Antonio sighs. "I was aiming for a tree. The car pulled to the right and went off the cliff. I had wedged her foot onto the gas so the crash would have looked good. No seatbelt, one hit to the forehead, it would have been believable. But nope, right off the cliff."

"Why didn't you call it in then?"

"I did!"

"Not until Monday!"

"The car went off the cliff right in front of a group of people! They were literally less than fifty yards away. It would have been impossible to miss unless they were smokin' crack! Hell, I saw two of them today hanging out in the parking lot of the motel."

"Yeah," I say, "something tells me those guys

weren't paying too much attention. What did you hit her with in the first place?"

"Crowbar."

"Why?"

"It's what I was supposed to do if she didn't give me the envelope? Duh."

"How did you even see her? I mean... How did you know where she would be? Or, how did you get her in the car and out to the cliff? There's no way you dragged her out of her apartment. That would be ridiculous."

Antonio shakes his head. "We had a meeting."

My fists are clenched so tightly my nails are digging into my palm. I've never had a more infuriating conversation. My phone chimes, but I ignore it.

"Why?!" I yell, letting out my anger in a rare display, although I suspect it's more frustration than anything.

"That's what I was told to do! I'm not lying to you."

"Who told you?" Archie asks, more calmly than I could have.

"You... really don't know?"

Argh!

"No! We really don't know."

Antonio is thinking about his answer, seemingly debating the pros and cons of telling us. "It was-"

Outside the window, a dark sedan pulls sideways through the parking spaces, slowing directly in front of us. The driver, a large bald man, aims a gun in our direction.

"Shit! Get down!" I grab Archie and pull him to the floor just as the shots ring out, and the glass shatters. The car's tires screech away. Antonio falls to the ground, half his head missing.

ERiC

Shit! I sent my mom a text, but it wasn't in time! The car is screeching away just like in those crappy 80's action movies we love so much, complete with the smoke and everything. It would be awesome if he weren't headed directly towards Jamie and Elliot.

"Get down!" I yell just as Jamie grabs Elliot by the shirt and throws him into the wall, narrowly missing the speeding car.

Mom and Dad bust out of the hotel room and run towards the street. "Is everyone okay?" Dad yells. Luckily they both seem fine. I totally panicked there for a minute.

Dad runs past us and says, "Milo, not a word to your moms!" then makes his way to Elliot and Jamie, Elliot still on the ground after being chucked into the wall.

We join them.

Jamie is picking up Elliot and dusting him off. "Are you okay, honey? I'm so sorry. I didn't mean to throw you against the wall. I just had to-"

Elliot interrupts her and wraps his arms around her so hard she lets out a little yelp.

Thank goodness everyone is okay, even though I can't help but feel a little jealous about Elliot's current situation, nestled comfortably between the boobs of Goddess Jamie.

I swear to god that son of a bitch is smirking at me, too.

My mom joins in the hug, wrapping her arms around both my brother and Jamie. "Thank you," she says.

Jamie smiles that beautiful smile of hers and says, "Did you think you just brought me along for my good looks?" My mom and her both laugh. Elliot is sandwiched in between them. I'm not sure he can even breathe right now.

Poor bastard. It's like, 8 o'clock and still about ninety degrees with a million percent humidity. If he doesn't get out of that hug sandwich soon, he's a goner.

That'll teach ya to smirk at me.

ARCHiE

The first thing Elise asked Gene when the sheriffs arrived was about Monica's protection at the hospital. And by *asked*, I mean that in the most aggressive way possible. I have a feeling that poor Gene would have had a dreadful night if he answered the question incorrectly.

Luckily for him, he stationed a man outside her hospital door almost immediately after we left. Good for him.

The shirtless idiots are hiding poorly behind a bush, watching all the action. Gene is questioning us about what happened, and we're giving him as many details as we feel comfortable giving.

When he turns his attention to Eric and Milo about what they have to say, I wave Jamie over.

"What's up?" she says.

"That guy, Antonio is his name now, not Chad."

"*Was* his name," she corrects me.

Jamie's deadpan delivery of that line, despite the fact there is a dead body fifty feet away, tells me that she has been hanging out with us too much... already.

"That is correct. *Was*. Anyway," I continue, "he drove and got some Burger King then parked somewhere in the back. While no one is looking right now, can you run around to the back of the motel and just check it out. If the car is unlocked, open it and grab whatever you can – glove compartment, console, you know..."

"And if it's locked?"

"You're probably against smashing the window, huh?"

"Doesn't seem smart while we're surrounded by cops."

"Okay. Just look around and see if there is anything of note. There probably won't be, but that thing is going to be towed away soon, so this is our only chance."

Jamie gives me a salute and says, "Aye aye," then takes off away from the cluster of sheriffs and around the building.

Gene has returned to us for more questions. Elise interrupts him and says, "Why did you call Monica a Jane Doe earlier?"

"Because her ID was fake."

"Her ID was fake?" Elise and I say together.

Elise adds, "What do you mean, fake?"

"I mean," Gene says, "whoever that woman is, her name isn't Monica Gargan. At least it wasn't before four or five years ago. Since then, sure, she's established a few lines of credit and things like that, but Monica Gargan ain't her name."

"Wait, wait," I say, "the ID is fake, or her name isn't Monica Gargan? If she has a fake ID, she isn't opening lines of credit or getting an apartment."

"I'm just telling you what I found out after a few minutes of searching for her."

"You realize someone can legally change their name for $39.95, right? That doesn't make her ID fake."

Gene is silent.

Elise presses on. "I mean, married women change their names all the time. I've changed my name. Are all our IDs fake, too?

"Um... I guess not."

God, who hired these people?!

"You called her a Jane Doe," Elise says, "despite having forms of identification that say her name is Monica. Why?"

Gene shrugs, and Elise has to hold herself back from punching him square in the teeth.

"We're going to go be with our kids," I say. "If you need us, we'll be right over there next to those guys with the homemade bombs hiding in the bushes."

"They seem more competent," Elise mumbles as we're walking away.

Another loud pop, like the one that blew up the

mailbox from before. This one much closer, and followed immediately by screams that draw the attention of everyone out in the parking lot.

One of the shirtless idiots is yelling, screaming, cussing like a sailor on leave, as blood is shooting from the stumps where his fingers used to be.

"My hand! My hand!" He's running through the parking lot, almost in circles, blood squirting like a wet firework, as everyone stares in disbelief.

"I'm suing! I'm suing everybody!"

This jackass lit one of his little bombs and forgot to place it where it was intended to go. So enthralled by the other stuff happening around him, it slipped his mind to properly dispose of the lit explosive he was clutching in his hand.

The kids are laughing, and I don't blame them. I would be laughing too, if I wasn't horrified at the sheer stupidity of what I am witnessing.

"Good thing there is already an ambulance here," Elise says, her face buried into her palm.

While the shirtless idiot is being tended to, I pull out my iPhone and dial Max's number.

Max was my childhood friend who works in the records department of the Bakersfield Police Department. When I say he was my childhood friend, I mean he was my only childhood friend, and that was based strictly on location. He lived across the street. Two of the most unpopular kids to ever walk the halls of school, me with my special classes and Max with his rattail and homemade tank-tops, we really had no choice but to be pals.

"Archie!" he answers.

"Hey, Max. Got a minute?"

"I'm driving home, plenty of time. The traffic here has steadily gotten worse since you left."

"I believe it. I need you to run a name for me. Actually, maybe two names."

"It'll have to be tomorrow. I'm gone for the day. Ever

since Covid, we have new safety protocols and-"

"Tomorrow would be fine. Just..."

"As soon as I get there. Got it. I've seen this movie before. Wait. Didn't you *just* move? What the hell are you doing needing me to run names?"

"Dude, this place is pure mayhem. I never imagined. I seriously just watched some guy blow his hand off on accident."

Max is laughing so hard I have to hold the phone away from my ear.

"Only you guys," he says. "I swear to god. How's that Jamie girl doing? She still single?"

Sigh.

"Yes, Max. You can talk to her when you come out to visit."

Poor Jamie.

"Anyway," I say, "about those names."

"Yeah, let me pull over real quick, hold on." The line goes quiet for about thirty seconds before he comes back on. "Okay, shoot."

"First name, and most important, is Antonio Russo."

"There might be one or two Antonio Russo's out there, ya know. It's not exactly an uncommon name. We got a residence?"

"He was driving a car with Florida plates, but he's probably not from Sunrise Cove or Cocoa because he had a suitcase with him. Palm Beach, maybe? Orlando? Miami? I don't know."

"Got it."

"Who else?"

"A girl named Monica Gargan, but we're unsure if that's her real name or not. She may be running from someone or something. Name change is possible."

"Name changes are not a problem for me, as long as they're done legally."

"Thanks, buddy, I've gotta jet. Please call me first thing in the morning."

"Can do. Remember, your morning is three hours

earlier than my morning, so don't panic if it's a little later than you were hoping."

"Understood."

"Oh, Arch?"

"Yeah?"

"One more thing. You said he *had* a suitcase..."

"Yes. Mr. Antonio Russo is recently deceased."

"Jesus Christ," Max says through more laughter. "How recently?"

"Speckles of his blood are drying on my brand new 2021 Superstars."

More laughter.

I'm annoyed. "I just bought these, dude. They don't even smell yet." Although, in this heat, they will soon.

"Only you, man. Only you."

Max has a history of not taking too many things seriously. Some guy's blood on my new shoes? Hilarious. Dead body? Comedy gold.

"Thanks. Talk tomorrow."

"Adios!"

"What the hell did I miss?" Jamie says while walking towards us.

"Oh my god," Elise says. "I almost got into a fight with Deputy Gene and one of the Bomb Boys blew his hand off."

Jamie laughs. "I was gone five minutes. I can't leave you kids alone at all."

"Any luck with the car?" I ask.

"It's back there, but it's locked. I looked through the windows but there was nothing but a bunch of fast food bags and trash."

"No big deal. Thanks." I look around for a second, scanning the area. "I'm not sure if we can leave," I say, "but I sure would like to get the hell out of here."

"Oh," Elise says, "we found out some more about our girl. Biggest thing is that her name might not really be Monica Gargan."

"What is it, then?"

"Not a clue. She may have changed it when she came to Sunrise. But we're not even sure of that. We're not sure of anything aside from she's a great drummer, loves high heels, and thinks Mitzi has nice veins."

Jamie laughs. "Nice veins? Is she a nurse?"

I wasn't paying much attention to their conversation, but that grabs my attention. "What do you mean?" I ask.

"Every time I donate blood or go for a routine checkup," Jamie says, "the nurse always compliments my veins. No one else has ever complimented them, so I just made a guess."

"A nurse," I mumble, more to myself than anyone. "How many hospitals do you think there are in Palm Beach?"

Elise and Jamie both shrug.

"One, probably," Elise says.

"Probably a hundred plastic surgery places, though," Jamie says. "They need nurses, too, right?"

"Not sure," I say.

"Did I make a good guess?" Jamie asks, smiling. "Do you think she's a nurse?"

"Could be, James. Could be. We might need to run to Palm Beach tomorrow."

"Dad!" Eric whines. "Aryam is coming tomorrow, remember?"

"Right."

Aryam is Eric's friend that he met on a cruise we took down here two years ago. As weird as it was, she turned out to be from our original hometown. Two months before we got our huge payday and decided to move everyone down here, she told Eric that she was moving to Florida. She's not in Sunrise Cove, but she's close enough that they can visit quite often. She's already been over a few times while we were moving in, but, I guess, she's supposed to be here tomorrow, too. I've forgotten, or I never knew. Either way, I play it off like duh, of course she's coming tomorrow.

"That's why," I say, "you guys aren't coming with

us." I look to Jamie and give her my best please face. She takes the hint.

"Yeah, guys," Jamie says to the boys, "I'm hangin' out at your house tomorrow."

"Thank you!" Eric says.

Eric passing up a potential adventure to hang out with a girl tells me that I am getting old... I mean, he's getting old. Him. Not me.

Sigh.

"Mrs. Lemons?" It's Gene, walking across the parking lot towards us. My wife turns and acknowledges him. "We, um..."

Gene holds out his hand to reveal a small listening device.

"We found this under the table in the vic's room."

"A bug?" Elise says, confused.

Gene nods. "Yes, ma'am. It seems someone was listening."

That explains the perfect timing of the shot.

Shit.

"Gene," Elise says, her tone much nicer towards him now. "We need one more favor. We need you to put a man at Monica's apartment complex."

"What? Why?"

"Because somebody out there is looking for something. Something worth killing over. And unless we find it before them, we'll never know what, and whoever is behind this will be a ghost."

"How many people do you think we have in our department?"

"Gene," Elise says, her friendly tone hardening a bit. "I don't care if you have to deputize the guy who just blew his hand off; you need to get someone out there to babysit. At least until the morning. Hell, drag your drunk boss out there and just prop him against the goddamn door."

"You're so mean," Gene says under his breath.

Elise grabs him by both shoulders and looks straight into his eyes. "I'm not mean, Gene."

"Mean Gene Okerlund!" Elliot yells behind us, referring to the legendary professional wrestling interviewer from the heyday of WWF, now WWE.

Trying her best to ignore the kids, who are now actively wrestling each other, Elise returns her attention to Gene. "I'm just trying to solve a case that requires your participation. Do you want to be a hero cop or a disgraced cop? Think about it long and hard."

Gene nods his head. "Do you have the address?"

"Yes, I do, Gene. Thank you." Elise writes it down on a piece of paper from her purse and hands it to him.

He nods again. "I'm only eighteen, you know."

"Then this would be a good way to prove yourself and take over the job from the drunken idiot you work for. Kay?"

More nods.

"Okay. Now go, Gene! Go! Call us if you need us. I put our numbers on there, too. Go!"

Gene runs off towards his squad car and Elise turns around, facing away from him, and gently closes her eyes and relaxes her body in an effort to calm her inner chi, or whatever it is those dumb hippies believe in.

"Now what?" Eric asks.

I bite my lip and think. I have no idea. Do we go home and sleep and start fresh tomorrow? Do we check on Monica's apartment, protect it until someone else takes over? Drive to hospitals in Palm Beach?

I have no idea.

I look to Elise, who is just as stumped as I am.

"I don't think there is anything else we can do tonight," she says. "I guess... shit. Go back home, I guess. Figure out a game plan. James, Jesus, we didn't bring you here so we could have a babysitter, but you don't mind watching everyone tomorrow?"

"Are you kiddin'?" Jamie says cheerfully. "These are my best buds."

She wraps her arm around Eric and his face turns bright red. I try not to laugh.

ELiSE

Jamie came over before dawn, before the boys were even awake, so we could get the earliest start possible. We drove by Monica's apartment first thing in the morning, just to check that someone was watching it. There was an empty squad car parked right out front, so I figured they had it covered. Our next stop is back to Palm Beach to shotgun hospitals, looking for anyone who might recognize Monica from the selfie I took outside The Gull. It's a long shot, but for right now, it's our only move.

"While we're here," Archie says as he's turning off A1A into Palm Beach, "we should give the money back to Sarah Benson. Wherever it came from, no one seems to be looking for it or missing it, and if you scam someone, it usually doesn't result in a briefcase full of cash. No doubt that it's dirty, but this is Florida, man. All the money is dirty."

"I thought you didn't believe in the mob and dirty money," I say playfully.

"Maybe a little. Who knows?"

"Right... Anyway, I agree. We can swing by on the way out of town. Just tell her we couldn't find anything. She needs it more than someone who can lose that much money and not seem to miss it."

"Maybe we can buy that truck, too."

"You're not buying that truck. It's a piece of crap."

"Maybe I like pieces of crap."

I googled hospitals in Palm Beach and discovered that there sure were a lot for such a small town. Archie pointed out that we saw someone blow his hand off last night in a motel parking lot, and his point is taken.

"Maybe we should stop by the sheriff's office again,

first. Ya never know."

"You never know what, exactly?"

"Someone might know who she is. The town is pretty small."

"You just want to try and be friends with that lady sheriff."

"What?" I say, mock shocked. "No, I don't."

"Yes you do," Archie says, laughing. "She was mean to you, and it annoys the shit out of you. I knew it from the second she first spoke to ya. I'm surprised you didn't bake her some cookies and give her one of those broken heart best friend lockets."

"Shut up. I don't want to be her friend."

"Yes, you do."

"Well, why was she so mean? We're women. We're supposed to stick together. Rude! Can we go?"

Archie laughs again and says, "Fine. But don't be mad if she's still awful to us."

"Fine. Deal."

The Palm Beach Sheriff's Department was relatively empty in the early morning hour, but there were still a few officers milling about. We managed to flag one down.

"Look who it is."

I recognize him as Martinez, the same guy that helped us last time we were here.

"Back again?" he asks.

"Yep!" I say in a friendly tone, hoping to woo him like I did last time.

"Can't say I'm disappointed by that," he says, returning my smile.

I can hear Archie's eyes rolling behind me.

"We were hoping to speak to Sheriff Castillo," I say while doing a flirty little shoulder move that used to get me out of a lot of trouble when I was a teenage runaway. It's worked ever since.

"Well," Martinez says, "she was just called out to a shooting at the church."

"A homicide at the church?" Archie says, joining the

conversation.

"Shooting... That's what the call came in as."

"Which church," I ask.

Martinez shrugs. "First Street Baptist or something. Down on First Street."

Archie and I look at each other, both quite surprised.

Martinez says, "You're not gonna... ya know... you're not gonna go there, right?"

I shake my head. "Of course not. Wouldn't think of it, my dear sir. It wasn't Uncle Sam again, was it?" This time I giggle a little. "*Are we gonna go over there?* Ha, silly man."

Shut up, Elise.

Leave the bullshitting to Archie.

This is embarrassing.

Martinez does a single *ha* laugh, looks at us like we're psychotic, then says, "Don't think it was Sam. Pretty sure this one is a suicide."

Pressing my luck, I ask, "Any news on that... I mean, the Uncle Sam guy? I mean, ha, just, ya know, curious."

You suck at this!

Stop!

Stop being such an Antonio.

"Don't think so."

"Any link between the victims."

"That's what we're working on right now, actually. Two of them used to work for the Palm Beach Gazette before it went out of business, but there is no real connection other than that. Hundreds of people have worked there over the years. Besides, the other two guys didn't work there, so, ya know..."

"Check and see if they were ever all on a jury together," Archie says.

"Yeah," Martinez says, "we thought of that after the third one. No dice. The second guy wasn't even registered to vote and not exactly legal in the country. So, nobody is calling him for jury services."

Hail Mary.

I pull out my phone and pull up the selfie of the band and me. I zoom in on Monica and show Martinez. "Ever seen her before?"

"Don't think so. No, sorry. Who is she?"

"Just my friend. No big deal. Thanks. We'll try back later this afternoon on our way out of town. Maybe she'll be back by then. If not, no big deal."

"Let me guess," Archie says while getting into the car. "We're going to First Street Baptist."

I do my shoulder thing and say, "Do you mind?"

"Nah."

Never fails.

ARCHiE

Just as Martinez said, there were a few squad cars in the church's parking lot, along with a mobile forensics van, which seemed odd for a supposed suicide.

Castillo sees us walking up and lulls her head to the left side, saying, "Not you guys again."

Elise, all smiles, says, "Us again. We were just in the neighborhood."

"Well, you can't be here, so march your skinny little ass right back out of here."

Elise smirks, unsure how to continue. Her plan of being besties with the Palm Beach sheriff is crumbling before her eyes.

"We were just driving by and saw you. Thought we would stop and offer our services."

"I don't need them, thanks."

Despite there being absolutely zero sincerity in Castillo's voice, Elise gives her a cheerful *you're welcome.*

We're the only bystanders, which is pretty rare. But I guess a church parking lot at 8 AM on a Wednesday is pretty dull.

"Suicide?" I ask, breaking the awkward silence. "My grandma dragged me to church a few times when I was little, so I totally understand."

Elise smacks my arm.

"No," Castillo says. "Murder. Again."

"Well," Elise says, "we're pretty good with murders. It's sort of our thing if you know what I mean." I catch her doing the shoulder thing. Oops

Sheriff Castillo sighs and walks around the car towards us. "Look, Perky Tits, this is normally a quiet town. We have our problems, sure, hell, half of this place is mob-run, but we don't have people opening fire on our streets. Miami, sure, but not here. I don't like it. I don't like it one bit. In fact, I'm pretty goddamn sick of it."

Elise shrugs. "We can offer our services. We won't take the credit. We don't... ya know... care about that. We care about people not dying."

Castillo seems to be seriously thinking it over. She's just about to say something when a lab nerd from the forensic van calls out to her while running towards us.

Castillo introduces him as De La Cruz, which I take as a good sign that she's opening up to us a little. For Elise's sake. I couldn't care less.

De La Cruz nods to us, then tells Castillo there is something she needs to see.

Castillo nods.

"We ran ballistics on the bullet like you said."

"And?" Castillo says, back to her normal snippy tone.

"It matches Uncle Sam."

Holy shit. Uncle Sam has struck again.

"Shit," Castillo says, snatching the bag holding the bullet away from De La Cruz. "That's two back to back. I thought we had another two weeks."

"Wait, wait," Elise says, "the guy in the car was killed by Uncle Sam? That's what you're saying?"

"Looks like it," Castillo says before storming away and dropping a steady stream of obscenities that would make Redd Foxx blush.

I look to Elise and shrug. "This doesn't fit his M.O. at all."

"As far as we can tell, there are no witnesses to this one, where the others seem like they were specifically designed so that witnesses would see who was doing it. Doesn't make sense."

Elise calls out to De La Cruz, who was halfway back to his van. Elise runs over to him. I follow.

"When did this happen?" Elise asks.

De La Cruz says, "Looks to be last night. 8ish maybe. The coroner will be able to give you a better idea of that. I'm just going by what I've picked up over the years. I'm guessing twelve to thirteen hours."

"Was there service here last night? On a Tuesday?"

"Doubt it, but this is a community center, too. That building over there has several rooms that are used from anything from Boy Scout meetings to AA. I assume he was either there for one of those or was meeting someone, and things went horribly wrong for him."

"What's his name?"

De La Cruz shakes his head. "I can't tell you that."

"Fair enough," Elise says. "Thank you for your help."

"No sweat. Um, who are you again?"

Elise cocks her thumb over her shoulder, pointing behind us, and says, "We... are late."

De La Cruz looks at us like we just stole his wallet but eventually turns around and walks back to his van.

"We need to see what they had going on in here last night?" I say, despite the fact we really need to hit the hospitals. Nothing like overloading your plate.

Speaking of plates, I'm starving.

"I bet the church is open. We can see if there is a schedule posted."

I nod. "And if it's not open, I might know of a way to get in."

"No moral qualms about breaking into a church?"

"None at all. Let's go."

It turns out I didn't need to flex my skills; the doors were unlocked. A long hallway divided two sides of rooms, like a school, just smaller. We make our way towards the front, peeking in every room along the way, coming up with nothing.

"This reminds me of a place my dad took me a million years ago."

"Church?"

I laugh. "No, that was my grandma, and it was once and only once, let me tell ya. Naw, he enrolled me in Boy Scouts when I was like ten or so, after I had started talking but still obviously had some problems. He thought it would be a good way for me to, ya know, get out somewhere that wasn't the *special classes* at school."

"It didn't work?"

"No. I had no idea what was going on. We stuck it out for a few weeks, but it was clear that I just did not fit in anywhere."

Elise grabs my arm and stops me. Hugging me, she says, "You fit in with me. Come on." She holds my hand, and we continue walking.

At the end of the hallway, a bulletin board displays several notices, and more importantly, a weekly schedule of events happening here. It's jam-packed.

I rip it off the wall, shove it in my pocket, and say, "Let's get out of here. I need some food."

"Yeah, we need to think this over."

ELiSE

"Ya know," Archie says, shoving a bagel in his mouth, "we could just forget this one. This isn't our problem. Like, at all."

"I know, but what are the odds of us being right here for two attacks in a row. Like, it has to be astronomical. It seems like the universe wants us to be involved in this."

"You and your universe. And I wouldn't call it astronomical. That seems like a bit of an overstatement."

"Oh, you know what I meant. Come on."

"We need to focus on Monica. She's still alive, remember. And as long as she's alive, and we haven't figured this nonsense out, she's in danger."

We're at a small diner a block inland from the beach. Archie is loading up a second bagel with cream cheese when two boys about Elliot's age approach our table.

"Hi," one of the boys says. Archie completely ignores them, still loading up the bagel.

"Hi," I say, smiling.

"Are you... Elise Lemons?"

Confused, I say, "Um, yeah?"

"Told you," the boy says to his friend. "Can I have your autograph?"

Completely confused now, I say, "Sure. Why?"

"You're famous," the boy says. "Look." He points to the TV where, sure enough, there I am in the parking lot of that motel. I was so consumed by everything happening I didn't even notice the press. "We've seen your movie like ten times. Nothing else was playing, but still. It was awesome."

"He thinks you're soooooooo cute," the other boy says, causing the first boy's poor face to turn redder than a tomato. "No, I don't!"

"He so does."'

"Shut up!" the first boy says, followed by a brief shoving match like boys are known to do.

Archie, with a full mouth, mumbles, "Awful lot of grab-assin' goin on here."

"H-O-T," the other boy says, still taunting his poor friend. They both totally ignore Archie.

"No," the kid says, "I mean, maybe, but that's not..." He takes a deep breath, trying to reclaim his cool. He hands me a pen and piece of paper, which I gladly take and sign.

"It's okay, kiddo. I think you're pretty cute, too," I tell him. He looks as if he's going to faint, and now I feel bad for saying anything.

Archie says, "You want mine, too, kid?"

"No thanks," the boy says before they both run off back to their table.

Archie gives me an annoyed smirk. I can't help but laugh.

"I think you're cute, too, ya know."

"Aw, honey," I say, "I think you're adorable."

He smiles. "K, just making sure."

While he eats his second bagel, I scan over the church's schedule. De La Cruz was right. The assortment of events taking place there was quite eclectic. There was an over-eaters group, a group for people with cancer, a group for people who lost loved ones due to the pandemic, a Boy Scouts group, a Girl Scouts group, and a rare coin collectors group.

In other words, nothing that helps figure out what the hell is going on.

I tell Archie, who says, "Maybe we should just give this one up. You're right. It's not our problem. Let's go hit the hospitals and see what we can find. That's a long shot, but at least it's constructive to the case we're actually working on."

He's right. Monica is our top priority right now. Maybe if we get her thing taken care of and they still need help with Uncle Sam, we can come back to it. But Archie is right. Not right now.

I nod.

Archie shoves almost an entire bagel in his mouth and mumbles, "Kay, let's go then."

ARCHiE

There are four major hospitals, not including one children's hospital, in the Palm Beach area. The amount of hospitals compared to the people in the city is ridiculous. There should be one, maybe two, but nope. Four. And those are just the main ones. I'm not even counting the several public and private urgent cares, surgery centers, Botox clinics, whatever.

We decide to start with the hospital closest to the sheriff's department and work our way out. Our goal is to, A: Find out what Monica's real name is since it doesn't seem to be Monica Gargan, B: Find out what she is running from so we can help, and C: Find out what is in an envelope, that she is presumably in possession of, that is so important it's worth killing.

And with no other leads right now, this is our only choice.

We walk into the first hospital, identify ourselves, then ask if we can speak to anyone that has worked here for more than five years, longer if possible. The woman working the front desk tells us that she has worked here for almost nine years.

Elise shows her the picture, but no luck. We ask four more people currently working, and they all tell us the same thing.

Nobody recognizes her.

Same with the second hospital

Same with the third hospital.

It's almost noon when we walk into the fourth, Memorial General, which seems like an odd name, considering most people want to go to a hospital to, ya know, not die. Memorial is what other people do after you kick off. If I owned a hospital it would be named High Five the Receptionist On Your Way Out General.

Seems a little more hopeful than Memorial. But hey, they don't ask me.

We explain our situation again to the guy at the front desk who says he's only worked here six months, but he knows some of the ladies have been here for decades.

"If they're not busy," Elise says, "can you maybe go get them. It's important, I promise."

The receptionist picks up the phone and pages... somebody. It's so jumbled and mumbled I can't make out a single word he says.

Whoever it was intended for must have understood, because two women in scrubs approach the front desk.

"My name is Elise and this is my husband, Archie. We're trying to track down our friend and were wondering if you could help us. We're pretty desperate."

Elise shows the pictures to the women, and one of them, the older one, says, "Oh."

"You know her?"

"Yeah," the nurse says. "Yeah, I know her."

I'm in such complete shock that this actually worked, I say, "You shittin' me?"

"No, sir," the nurse says. "That's Monica."

"Hey!" Elise says. "Yes!"

"Do you remember her last name?" I ask.

The nurse thinks for a moment, then answers, "No. First name is Monica, though. Her hair is a lot longer now, but other than that, she almost looks exactly the same. Good for her."

"Do you remember if her last name was Gargan?" Elise asks.

"Hmm. No, that's not it. Doesn't sound familiar, at least. I'll think of it eventually."

"Can you tell us anything about her?" I say.

"I thought you said you were her friends," the nurse says.

"We are. We're trying to find her, and any information you give us could be vital to our search."

Sometimes I throw in words like *vital* to really make

me sound official.

"Well," the nurse says, "she... Do you know about what happened to her here? I'm assuming you do since you came here."

"Like my husband said, Miss..."

"Reynolds."

"Oh my gosh," Elise says. "That's my maiden name."

Two Monicas and now two Reynolds? It's like my life is being written by some hack writer that doesn't know what a random name generator is.

"Please tell us all you know, Miss. Reynolds," I ask. "We are in a desperate hurry."

"Excuse me, guys," Reynolds says to her coworkers. She tells us to follow her to the small waiting room. We do. When we were a safe distance away from being overheard, she says, "Monica got herself into a bit of trouble when she was here.

"She worked for a doctor named Clements. He proved to be... less than ethical, let's say. Did a lot of shady deals, shady work, shady payments."

"Can you elaborate on that a little?"

Reynolds looks over her shoulder, making sure the coast was clear. Regardless of there being no one around, she still lowers her voice. "He was doing surgeries that were never reported, or they were reported as something minor when it may have been something major, and, ya know, taking cash payments, showing patients out the rear exit... get it?"

"I'm assuming he got caught," I say. "But do you know where we can find him?"

"Yeah," Reynolds says. "Try the cemetery."

"Shit."

"He died in prison a few years back. Your girl, however, you didn't hear this from me, did five years. I heard when she got out she left town, and until about ten minutes ago, I hadn't seen nor thought of her since."

"What did she get busted on?" Elise asks.

Reynolds shrugs. "She got a lesser sentence than the doc, but I think the judge really threw the book at both of them. Doc got fifteen years but only lasted four. Monica served her sentence, got out a year early, then poof. Gone."

"So," Elise asks, "was Monica this Doctor Clements' personal nurse?"

Reynolds nods, her lips pursed together.

"The mystery deepens," I say to Elise. "Thank you so much for your help. I don't have a card, but let me write down my number for you. If you happen to remember her last name from back then, or anything, please give us a call."

"Sure," Reynolds says. "So she got out and changed her last name, I assume?"

"Looks that way," Elise says, writing our number on a piece of paper and handing it to Reynolds. "Thank you so much for your help."

"You sure she didn't just get married?"

Elise smiles. "Yeah, that would have made things a lot easier, believe me."

"Yeah," I say, ready to go. "Anyway, we really appreciate it."

"I hope you find her. She was a good kid. I blame Clements, not her. She didn't know. She should have gotten a slap on the wrist and sent home."

"One more thing," I say. "Do you know who any of the clients were that got this special treatment?"

Reynolds shakes her head no. "That was all very hush-hush."

"It never came out?"

Another head shake. "Not even at the trial. Nobody said a word. That's probably why they got punished so harshly."

"Thank you again," Elise says. "You've been an incredible help."

"I hope you find her, and I hope she's okay. Let her know she still has at least one friend at Memorial."

"We'll do that. Again, thank you."

We're halfway to the car when my phone rings.

Max.

It's been such a busy morning I've almost forgotten all about him.

"Maxwell," I answer, "what ya got for me?"

"Well, good morning to you, too."

Sigh. "Good morning, Max! You're on speakerphone with Elise, too, so please no crudeness."

"Oh, why hello, lovely Elise."

"Hi, Max."

Elise isn't the biggest Max fan, but she's warmed to him a bit over the years. Max used to have a way of being, well, offensive. And sexist. Which he defended by always saying he was just kidding. That might work for children, but not so much for a forty-year-old man who lives in a one-bedroom apartment with two cats.

"So," I say, trying to get back on track, "whatcha got for me?"

Max laughs and says, "You ready for this?"

"I'm ready."

"I don't know what you've gotten yourselves into, but Antonio Russo, that's his real name."

"Yeah, he was using the name Chad when we first met him. We got Russo later on."

"Well, if it's the same Antonio Russo, and I'm betting it is, he is... was... the nephew of one Frank *Mongo* Giuseppe."

"No way!" Elise yelps. "No. Way!"

"Looks that way, my dear. His mother, Antonio's, I mean, is serving twenty years up in Jersey Correctional for Women."

"What about his dad?"

"His mom killed him. That's why she's in the clink."

The clink. What is this, a 1960's cop show?

"Holy shit, Max. Mongo just washed up on shore here."

"Yeah," Max says. "I saw that. I don't know how you guys always manage to step into the biggest piles of shit, but you never miss."

"What about Monica?"

"I'll work on her. It takes a little more effort for name changes."

"It's fine. It doesn't seem that important anymore."

"You sure?"

"If you have time, go for it, but..."

"I get it. I'll be in touch."

"Thanks, Max."

"Hey, it's what I do. Introduce me to some Floridian babes when I come to visit."

"Sure thing!"

That's something I probably won't be doing.

I end the call and look at Elise, who is looking at me with her mouth open, wide-eyed.

"I know. I know."

ELiSE

The news about Antonio being Mongo's nephew is surging through my body like a wildfire. I knew there was more to that guy. There had to be. Now we just need to find out what.

Whatever is in this mystery envelope Antonio was looking for will probably provide a pretty big clue as to what the hell is going on.

We have to find it as soon as possible.

Archie says, "We need to drop that money off at Sarah Benson's house and tell her to enjoy her newfound wealth."

I agree, but I still want to get back home as quickly as possible and figure this all out.

Archie must see the anxiousness on my face. "It'll be ten minutes, don't worry."

"I'm not worried," I say, barely able to sit still in my seat.

"Maybe I'll buy that truck."

"Oh my god, you're not buying that piece of crap. It has no dash."

"It does have a dash. What do you think the duct tape is holding together?"

This guy makes me laugh so much.

Archie knocks on Sarah's door. I've had her money in my purse since I took it what seems like six months ago. We've had a hectic couple of days.

When Sarah opens the door, she greets us with a smile. She's still in her robe, coffee mug in hand, when she invites us inside. She's shaking slightly. I wouldn't even have noticed, but I can see the coffee rippling.

"We've called around and done some digging," I tell her, "and we can't find anyone who seems to be missing this money. I'm not saying it isn't illegally possessed. I'm just saying we can't seem to find who it was possessed from."

"And honestly, with your husband dead," Archie says, "I don't think anyone will come looking for it."

"If they haven't by now," I say, "then, I mean, the odds are pretty slim. That much cash going missing - seems like someone would either miss it right away, or never."

"And," Archie says, "the fact that it's in a briefcase that you say neither you nor your husband owned tells me this may have been a payoff of some sort. For what? I have no idea. And maybe it's better if you don't know. Maybe it's from a football pool, maybe it's from insider trading that he was a part of. The point is, you don't need to know. If you have no moral qualms about keeping it, just keep it. If you feel guilty, turn it in.

"But, if you turn it in, you'll probably lose it. Even if no one claims it, things like that have a tendency to go missing, if you catch my drift."

"The choice is yours, Sarah," I say, putting my hand on her shoulder. "No judgments here."

"What would you do?" she asks quietly.

"I've been in rough spots before," I say. "I know what you're feeling right now. Trust me. I know you'll make the right decision for what is best for you. You don't need us to tell you what to do."

"Regardless of what you decide," Archie says, "we won't tell a soul. So consider yourself the only person that knows about this. Okay?"

Sarah cups her mug with both hands and nods. To herself, she says, "Oh Carl, what did you do, you big dummy?"

"We've got to get going," I say. "We wish you the best of luck, Sarah. Thank you for trusting us."

We're walking back to the street, Sarah standing in the doorway watching us go. Archie is eyeballing the truck, thinking I don't notice him, when he stops dead in his tracks.

"What's wrong?"

No answer. He's just standing there, staring at Carl's old truck.

"Babe?"

Still no response.

I look back at Sarah, who is just as confused as I am. All three of us are perfectly still now, like some Wild West showdown.

Archie snaps out of it and jogs to our car, checking the back tire. "No mark."

"Huh?" I ask.

"The chalk mark. The X. It's gone."

"Of course, it's gone. It's chalk, *not spray paint.* Remember, I wiped it off with my shoe?"

"But it was faded, right? Like, almost gone anyway."

"Yeah..."

"Look," Archie says, running back towards the truck. He points to the back passenger's side tire. "X"

Sure enough. There is a chalk X on the tire.

"Sarah," Archie says a little too loud. "When was the last time Carl left the house?"

"I don't remember the exact date. Two weeks before he died. It must have been the Tuesday the week before he died."

"Why is that?"

"His meetings were on Tuesdays. The support group."

Holy shit.

"And where were his meetings?"

"The church. Um, First Street Baptist. Why?"

To me, Archie says, "The days are all a blur. When was the shooting at the park?"

"Monday."

"Monday..."

"Archie," I say, unsure of what is happening, but my body is so excited that I'm trembling. "What the hell does this mean?"

"That meter maid said the shooting that she missed

by a few minutes was on a Tuesday, not a Monday like the one was this week."

"Yeah..."

"That means Carl was in the vicinity of the third Uncle Sam attack."

"Why? How?"

"The chalk mark. That thing would have faded away into nothing if he had driven it. Ours came off completely after one day with just a tap of your shoe and was already faded by the time we even got home the day we got it. His X looks like it's brand-spankin' new. The last thing Carl Benson did before packing it in and staying home was *not* attend a support group. It was putting on an Uncle Sam mask and murdering a man leaving his office."

Sarah crumbles on the front porch, sobbing.

"Come on, E," Archie says, completely ignoring the suffering of poor Sarah and already getting in the car, "we need to go see the meter maid, again."

"What? How do we find her?"

"She works that route Monday through Friday, 7:30-5:30, remember?"

"We can't just leave poor Sarah like this?"

"Huh, why not?" Archie asks genuinely.

I run to Sarah and kneel next to her, wrapping her in my arms. "Sarah, honey, we need to get you inside. Do you have a friend you can call to stay with you?"

She's not listening to me at all.

"Sweetie, I need you to pay attention. Do you have a friend that can come stay with you?"

Eventually, she nods yes, and I help her to her feet and back inside.

"I knew it," she says through sobs. "I knew it. I was so stupid. Of course. Of course."

"Please call your friend. We will be in touch. I'm so sorry."

"Carl. You stupid son of a bitch!"

I lead her to her chair and sit her down.

"Why?" she asks, looking up at me, helpless.

"Maybe he did it to help you."

"That stupid, stupid man."

"Listen, call someone to come be with you. We need to go. I promise we'll be in touch."

I'm waiting for her to give me some sign that I'm okay to leave. She's just staring ahead now. I wanted to help her, but honestly, I don't have the time.

I'm just about to turn and leave when she says, "He could... he could be wrong. Right? Your husband?"

"Sure," I lie, putting my hand back on her shoulder. "Of course he could be."

ARCHiE

Shit.

Shit shit!

Shit shit shit!

We need to get back home and figure out Monica's problem. Why is nothing ever easy for us?

"Will you please tell me what the hell is going on?" Elise says impatiently as I try to navigate back to Chrissy's circle of hell.

"There is no way," Elise says, louder this time, "her husband is Uncle Sam. Sam killed someone this morning."

"Last night."

"You know what I mean."

"You've seen *Scream*! And *Scream 2*. And *Scream 3* and *4* for that matter."

It doesn't take her long to figure out my point. "Multiple Uncle Sams?"

"Multiple Uncle Sams."

"But why? Who?"

"Do you still have the schedule we took from the church?"

"Yeah." She reaches into her shorts' pocket and pulls it out.

"What meetings were last night? Tuesday the second."

Elise looks the paper over then says, "Boy Scouts and Cancer Support. I don't..."

"I think someone is paying terminally ill people to be hitmen."

"What? That's insane. What about the guy this morning?"

"You saw him. That guy probably looked just as dead before the bullet entered him. He was gaunt as shit. I'm thinking he was approached about a job, and things didn't go the way they were supposed to."

"So you think Sarah's husband was approached the same way?"

"Yeah. I think someone is infiltrating support groups, picking out the people who have questionable morals or lack of faith in a higher power, and making them an offer they can't refuse.

"Think about it. Sarah said it herself. Carl wasn't religious at all. If you don't believe in the afterlife, and you have just the right amount of anger or bitterness, you might be convinced to do a job that could support your family, or in this case, his wife, long past his death.

"Maybe this guy convinced Carl and the others that the people they were killing deserved it. You never know. But there is definitely a link between them all. No way someone is paying for hits on a bunch of randoms."

"Dude," Elise says with a sigh. "What a week."

"What a week indeed."

"It won't always be like this. We're going to be relaxing on the beach in no time."

I'm not a big fan of beaches. I enjoy looking at them from afar, I love the salty air, the breezes, the smell... but being on the actual beach has not been something I've ever been a fan of. Especially on the sand. But at this exact moment, sitting in a folding chair, the ocean in front of me, Elise at my side, the kids doing whatever it is they do, sounds like the best thing in the world to me.

"You know," Elise says, "*Scream 3* didn't have two killers."

"Bah! Whatever. *Scream 3* sucks. Not enough Sidney."

"There she is!" Elise shouts, pointing to Chrissy with her stupid chalk wand.

I pull to the curb, double-parked and blocking the lane.

"Hey!" Chrissy yells at us. "What the hell, man?"

Elise throws her arms up in a *'we come in peace'*

sort of way and says, "We need your help."

"What?" Chrissy says confused, but still managing to taunt me with that goddamn chalk stick.

"Do you have briefcases full of money?"

"What the heck are you talking about? Briefcases full of money? And I'm walking around in the scorching heat in this outfit handing out tickets? Good one."

"Damn."

"Archie," Elise says, her palms upturned, looking at me in utter disbelief.

"Sorry. Look," I say, "we need to know everything about the Uncle Sam killing that took place on your route."

"I told you all I know. And that's nothing aside from it being Tuesday the 18th at around 4:30."

"You were here when it happened?"

She shakes her head. "No, I was way back on the other street. Back where you guys parked the other day. God, did you forget everything I told you?"

"But you were on duty? You were actively marking cars?"

"Yeah. I already told you that. What's this all about?"

"Do you remember marking a beat-up old truck?"

She laughs. "You kidding?"

"We might have a lead on who is doing this," Elise says. "And you could be very helpful."

"Oh geez, okay. What do you need?"

"We have to go," I say. "We have something equally important to do back home. You said the other day that two of the victims used to work for the same paper, but the other two didn't, which meant there was no link between the four. Yeah?"

"Yeah."

"Do you know what paper it was? Martinez told us, but I can't remember."

"Yeah. It was the Palm Beach Gazette, but it's not even a thing anymore. I only know that because it was the only paper we had that was semi-local. I think they have a website now, but the actual paper has been gone for at least five or six years."

"We need you to find Sheriff Castillo and tell her you talked to us. She might act like she's annoyed, but whatever. Tell her we need to find out when those two victims worked at the paper. I'm willing to bet there was some overlap."

"Okay," Chrissy says nervously. "I... I can do that, sure."

"Then we need you to find out who else worked there at the same time of the overlap that is wealthy now. Wealthy enough to pay off large sums of cash to people. We're talking hundreds of thousands of dollars."

"How the hell do I do that?"

"Someone will be able to figure it out," Elise says.

"But... why? Only two of the four were..."

"I'm going off a hunch. We worked a case once where a guy killed his wife then kept on killing other random women in the guise of a serial killer to draw suspicion away. Maybe there is somebody at that paper, or who used to be there, that is holding a major grudge."

"So you think he's knocking off innocent people mixed with the people he really wants to kill? That's awful."

"It's even worse. I think he's paying terminally ill people to do it for him. After the shooting, you saw no trace of the shooter?"

"No. I was told he ran down one of the alleys and escaped. You're saying he was terminally sick?"

"I believe so."

"How did he get away then? I would think someone that was sick wouldn't be able to just hightail it out of a crime scene."

"I'm sure everything was meticulously planned, even down to the route he took and the time of day. A hundred thousand dollars is a pretty big motivator."

"Oh my god," Chrissy says, covering her mouth with her left hand.

"Yeah. The mask and shirt were easy to tear off. He

hid them somewhere, along with the gun, to be picked up by the guy who hired him later and passed on to the next poor dupe. Nobody bothered to look for the costume or the gun because they assumed he held on to it to use the next time."

"This is incredible."

"Can you do us this favor, Chrissy?" Elise asks.

"Yeah... Yes. Of course. I'll go right now."

Elise is writing our names and numbers down on another piece of paper and handing it to the meter maid. "As soon as you find anything out. Okay?"

"I'm on it."

"Thank you."

ELiSE

I called Jamie on the car ride back home to fill her in on everything we learned. Hearing me say it all out loud just made it sound completely absurd.

If I weren't there, I certainly wouldn't have believed it.

Jamie said things were fine at home and that all the kids were playing out back. She had a full house, as our place has become the designated hangout spot.

She told us to be careful, assured us that Gary was safe and happy right next to her, and to call if we needed anything. I thanked her and hung up.

Our first stop back in town was Monica's apartment. We pull into guest parking and take the spot right next to the squad car. I'm happy to see someone has been guarding this place since we left.

We desperately need to see what is inside this mystery envelope that seems to be so popular.

When we approach her building, we see a deputy sitting in a folding chair, literally right outside Monica's door.

"Howdy," the female deputy says to us as we approach.

"Hey," I respond. I need to get rid of this woman so we can break back into the apartment and ransack it further. "Thanks for guarding the place. Any action?"

"Oh, you must be the folks that needed this place watched. Gene told me all about it."

"That's us. You been out here all night?"

"Nope. I got here about an hour and a half ago. Took over duty from another fella."

"No action?"

"Not a thing."

"That's what we like to hear. We really appreciate

your help. We can take over from here. I'm sure Gene needs you back at the station."

"You don't need me anymore? Man, this job was great."

"I hear that. But yeah, we're here now to take over."

"I better call the sheriff and see if I'm allowed to just go."

"Do what you've gotta do. Tell him it's Elise and Archie Lemons."

Archie pulls out his wallet and flashes his Montana driver's license.

Hopefully, it's still early enough for Sheriff Murray to comprehend what is going on, but who am I kidding.

The deputy makes the call then says, "It's all yours, guys. Good luck. Hell, I don't even know what I'm doing here." She laughs. "Easy money."

When she's safely out of the way, Archie picks the lock, and in we go. I open up the front curtains to let in some more light. If anyone questions us now, at least we have a plausible explanation for being here, unlike before.

The place has been searched pretty well, at least at first glance. All the drawers are out and flipped, the fridge is empty, the few jars in the pantry are opened and thrown on the floor. The cushions are cut to ribbons, the carpet pulled up at the edges.

I decide to search the tile in the kitchen. I'm pushing on each individual one, looking for a falsie. When that doesn't pan out, I pick up a screwdriver from one of the tossed drawers and begin removing all the electrical outlets and light switch covers.

Nothing there.

"Anything?" I yell to Archie, who is searching the bedroom."

"Jack-dick nothing!"

The kitchen is thoroughly searched. Nothing left to find in there, so I sit on the floor and gather up a group of pens that were dumped. I unscrew them and check the insides. We have no idea how big the envelope is or what it holds. It could be something tiny, and maybe rolling it up in a pen would serve as a good hiding spot.

No luck there, either.

I peek my head into the bedroom. "I checked everything out here. And I mean everything. Nothing at all. I even pulled the pens apart to see if there was anything rolled up."

"Yeah, I'm having no luck in here either."

"We didn't check her car. I mean, it's worth a shot."

"Yeah. Let's check the bathroom and the drains, just in case."

"Of course."

We move into the bathroom. Archie is searching the drains, the toilet tank, the tiles, while I remove the two switch plates from the wall. Still nothing.

"We can pull out the medicine cabinet. Most people don't realize those are easily removed."

"Good idea."

Archie opens the medicine cabinet's mirrored door first, checking what is in there. It looks like a box of tampons, some toothpaste, floss, Tylenol, and some nail polish remover. Archie holds the medicine, looks at me, and shrugs. "Worth a shot."

He twists the lid off the bottle and looks inside. Just pills. I grab the tampon box and open it. There are four left. I dump them out into my hand and see that one is opened at the bottom.

My body starts tingling.

I pull the wrapper back and find a piece of blue film, folded in half and rolled as tightly as possible. "Holy shit."

"Elise Lemons for the win!"

I unroll the film. Not film at all. An x-ray.

"What the hell is that?"

"Got me." I hold it up to the light, but I can't make heads or tails out of the picture. Something does catch my eye, though. The name that's printed on the far right.

Francis Giuseppe.

—

"I told you!" I practically yell while jumping up and down. "I knew it!"

"Strange things are afoot at the Circle K. We got what we needed, now let's get the hell out of here."

I fold the X-ray back along the original crease and shove it in my shorts pocket, and then we make our way back to the living room, where we see a large burly bald man standing right outside the window holding a Molotov cocktail, lit and ready to go. Archie and I stop dead in our tracks, staring at the goon that shot Antonio, the same dead look in his eyes.

He cocks his arm back and lets loose his explosive aimed right for us.

ARCHiE

We have no time to move, everything seems to happen in slow motion, but what we witness is one of the dumbest things I have ever, or will ever, see.

It seems our friend used a plastic two-liter bottle for his Molotov cocktail, and when it hits the window directly in front of us, it bounces right back to him, igniting him instantly and engulfing his entire body in flames. If you've ever seen *Maniac Cop*, then you know. My mouth is wide opened. I'm so wholly dumbfounded my brain can't even tell my feet to move. Elise, apparently doing better than me, runs to the bedroom and grabs Monica's comforter, then runs back past me. This snaps me out of my brain fog, and I follow her out just as she uses the large blanket to tackle the Goon. His screams have brought everyone in the area out to see just what the hell was going on.

The Goon hits the ground, still screaming, still on fire. I help Elise, trying to pat him off to little avail. The stream is about ten feet behind him, so with the comforter as a shield, albeit a shitty one, we push his body over and roll him into the water. He sizzles like a fajita platter.

"Holy shit!" I yell. "Are you okay?"

Elise nods. "I'm okay. Are you okay?"

From a balcony somewhere, someone yells, "I called 911!"

Everyone else has their phones out, filming this instead of actually helping, including some frat-boy douchebags making some highly inappropriate comments about Elise being hot.

My man in the stream, however, is steaming.

Steamin' and screamin'.

Steamin' and screamin' in the streamin'.

"Sit tight, buddy," I say to our would-be atttacker, "help is on the way." I begin searching his pockets, looking for anything that may be of use to us. He's too out of it to even notice. "Why... Why would you use a plastic bottle? That doesn't even... that doesn't even make sense, dude."

I find his phone and remove it from his front right pocket. It's a little wet and a little warped, but it'll be fine. "Hey, what's your password for this?" I hold it right in front of his face. "Stay with me. What's the password? I need it to call for help?"

I'm hoping he's too loopy to notice my blatant lie.

With what sounds like an awful lot of pain and hardly any lip movement, The Goon mumbles, "6969."

"How clever. Thanks. Help is coming. Stay with us, homes. We need you to stay with us."

His eyes start to flicker and rollback.

"Stay awake," Elise says. "Someone is coming to help. What's your name? Can you tell me your name?"

Goon tries to open his lips to speak but quickly thinks better of it. They're practically melted together.

"It's okay," Elise says, getting on her knees so he can see her. "We're right here, okay. We're right here."

"We found the X-ray," I say. "So all this was for nothing, dude. You saw us in there. You have no problem throwing a fireball at my wife, dude? Shit!"

Elise gives me a look, telling me to be quiet. She's a better person than me.

"We have kids, dude," I say, making sure he can see me, flickering eyes or not. My sympathy is fading fast the more I think about the alternative to this situation. Elise, however, has taken a seat on a small rock next to him, her shoes in the water. She's trying to comfort him. In the distance, sirens grow louder and louder.

When the paramedics arrive, the same guys as before, Elise shows them the X-ray, but they don't waste any time looking at it. One guy says it looks like the back of a skull, then quickly hustles away to get Goon loaded up and shipped off.

The sirens start to blare again as the ambulance tears out of the parking lot like they've got someone in the back that *didn't* just try to murder us.

We're about to walk back to our car and drive to the nearest doctor's office for an appraisal of the X-ray when we hear tires skidding through the parking lot. Sheriff Murray is pulling into the lot. He crashes into the goddamn curb before getting out and stumbling towards us, somehow managing to step on a squirrel. Poor little thing popped like an overfilled water-balloon. I can hardly believe my own eyes.

Elise is repulsed.

Murray didn't even notice. "What the hell happened here?" he slurs.

"Little early on a Wednesday to be tripping over your own feet," Elise says. "Don't ya think?"

"It'th the Forth ofth July! I'm sssselabratin'."

"Two things," Elise says. "It's not the Fourth of July, and, um, you're on duty and driving. Oh my gosh, that reminds me! Quick, let me see your keys!"

Murray smiles like he just won a prize, then hands Elise his keys.

"Thanks," Elise says. "Watch this magic trick." She dangles the keys on her finger in front of Murray's glassy eyes. "Abra kadabra!"

A confused Murray asks, "What'th the trick?"

Elise smiles and says, "This," while chucking the keys on the roof of Monica's building. To me, she says, "Let's go, babe."

I arch my eyebrows at him and say, "See ya, Murray. Happy holidays, ya bastard."

ELiSE

We decide that the hospital will be the easiest place to find a doctor, any doctor, rather than looking for private practices. We basically followed the ambulance.

I slip my wet ankle boots back on with absolutely zero grace and enter the small ER through some sliding doors and get our temperatures checked, which is something they still do here, I guess, then head on in. A lady asks if she can check us in, and we tell her our situation.

"Oh, ok," she says, somewhat confused. "Head through the ER and into the hospital. Someone will be able to help you better there, okay. You guys smell yummy. Did you just come from a BBQ? I'm starving."

Archie laughs. "Something like that. Grilled asshole."

"Oh," the receptionist says, "I love hot dogs."

We cut through the ER and back into a hospital waiting room. A woman with a blonde ponytail and scrubs walks past us, so I say, "Excuse me, I'm sorry."

She turns to look at us, eyebrows raised. "Yes?"

"Are you a doctor?"

"I am."

"Can we have two minutes of your time if you're not busy?"

"What'd you need?"

"You won't even believe the story, but just trust us when I say this is very, very important." I take the X-ray out of my pocket and show it to her. "Can you tell us what this is?"

"It's an X-ray," she says with a laugh. "I'm kidding. Come on, follow me."

We follow her into an examination room, and she

hangs the X-ray up on a light board.

"This," she says, "is the back of someone's head."

"Anything special about it?" Archie asks.

"Yep. This warped little square here... that's a metal plate."

"What does that mean?" I ask.

"It means your patient here had something happen to his skull that required a metal plate to be installed to avoid any further damage."

"What could have caused the damage, Doc?" Archie says.

"Anything really; A car accident, a fall, botched kickflip on a skateboard down a flight of stairs, hit by a baseball if it was pitched hard enough... there's no way to say for sure. Any blow to the skull can potentially cause damage."

"You have a patient here named Monica Gargan. Do you know her?"

Doc pulls the X-ray from the board and says, "I'm assuming that's the Jane Doe that came in."

I roll my eyes and say, "Yeah. The deputy didn't understand... well, that's beside the point. Does she have someone posted outside of her door?"

"She does, yes."

"Okay, good. How... is she?"

"She's steady. Steady brain activity. She a friend?"

"Very much so."

Doc nods her head sympathetically and says, "We'll just have to wait it out and hope she wakes up. I'm hopeful."

"I'm sure you're doing all you can for her. We appreciate it."

Doc is just about to hand us the X-ray back when she notices the name. "Francis Giuseppe?"

Uh oh.

"Mongo? The mob guy that... Who did you guys say you were again?"

Archie reaches over and snatches the X-ray from the doctor, and says, "Yoink!"

———

"Gotta go, Doc!" I say as we make our speedy exit from the room. "Thank you!"

"Hey!"

We cut left, back through the ER, hoping to avoid anyone that may have been sent to get us, although I'm sure we're overreacting. We just don't have the time to spare for any hiccups or hold-ups.

In the car and safely away from the hospital, Archie says, "A metal plate? I don't get it."

"I think I might have an idea. We need to call the Palm Beach Sheriff's Department. Or, more specifically, Sheriff Castillo."

"Cool, you guys are besties now, so it shouldn't be a problem."

"Come on. When was the last time we saw a female in any sort of authoritative role? It was refreshing. I'm sick of men."

Archie laughs. "Oh no, I totally get it. You see that drunken idiot stumble out of his car?"

I'm laughing now. "What a disappointment he turned out to be."

"Dude, when you threw the keys on the roof. Goddamn. Chef's kiss. Bravo."

I take my seatbelt off and kiss my husband on the lips. We've had a hell of a time these past couple days, and I'm so happy he's been by my side through all of it.

"What was that for?"

"Oh, you know. 'Cuz I love you."

"That's good news because I happen to know this guy that loves you, too."

"Oh yeah? Is he cute?"

"Eh. Bit of a dad bod type of guy that still dresses like he's in his early twenties."

"This is great news because that's exactly the type of fella I go for! What a day!"

"What a day indeed!"

"Come on. We need to make a call."

"It was me, you know. I was talking about me."

"Someone get M. Night Shyamalan on the phone for that twist!"

"Leave him alone. He's making a comeback."

"Oh, totally," I say, finding the number for the Palm Beach Sheriff's Department. "Hold on."

"For sure."

I dial the number and wait for three rings before a gruff-voiced man picks up.

"Palm Beach Sheriff's Department."

"Hi. This is Elise Lemons. We were there earlier, actually. I need to talk to Sheriff Castillo if she is available?"

"Is it important?"

"Very much so."

"Hold on."

I picture this guy as a too-big-for-his-chair type, chomping on a stinky cigar and with stubble so rough you could strike a match on it.

I could be wrong, though.

"Castillo."

Oh wow. Wasn't expecting that. "Hi, Sheriff. It's Elise Lemons."

I think I hear a sigh, but I'm not positive. Regardless, I press on.

"Did Smith get in touch with you? The meter maid?"

"She did, yes." After a brief pause, she says, "That's good work. If it's correct."

"Thank you. We'll be down there again real soon, but in the meantime, um, you remember the body that washed up on the shore of Sunrise Cove?"

"Frank Giuseppe? The mob boss that gave me seven pounds of paperwork and a shellacking from the feds? Yeah, Ms. Lemons, I seem to recall."

Mrs. Lemons, but I don't correct her. "Um yeah, him. Um. You said the feds came to get him, yeah?"

"Of course they did. You don't think they would let little ol' us handle something like that, do you?"

"When did they come? Was there an autopsy done first?"

"Yeah," she says, sounding more and more annoyed with each passing second. "They gave us the privilege of doing all the leg work before swooping in to take credit. I guess they had to be sure it was worth their precious time to come down here."

"So one of your men or women did the autopsy?"

"That's correct."

"Can you, maybe, tell me the name of the person that did it?"

Another sigh, this one strictly for my benefit. "Why?"

"I might have a way you can stick it to the feds and get way more credit than you ever thought."

Another brief moment of silence. "I'm listening."

"I just need the name and contact info for whoever did the autopsy. And for you to tell him he's free to speak openly to us."

"Her. Not him."

This makes me smile. "Sure, of course. Her."

"You gonna be around for a few minutes?"

"I'm not going anywhere."

"She's here. I'll have her call you in a few minutes. Good enough?"

"Good enough. And thanks."

"Yeah," she says, then ends the call.

To Archie, I say, "She'll call us back."

The look on his face tells me he won't be holding his breath. "So you wanna get some food or something?"

"I guess I could eat."

"That's my girl."

"Shit, hold on." My phone is ringing again. "It's Castillo."

"Wow," Archie says. "Impressive. Most impressive."

"Hi," I answer way too bubbly. I forget that this isn't one of my real friends.

"Is this Elise?" a female's voice asks. Not Castillo.

"It is, yes."

"This is Valentina Vasquez, the medical examiner at the Palm Beach Sheriff's Department."

"Oh wow, thank you so much for getting back to me, Ms. Vasquez. Did you do the autopsy on Francis Giuseppe?"

"I did."

"How... Um. How did you know it was him? I mean, how did you know that bloated corpse was Frank Giuseppe?"

"How did I personally figure it out? Or how did the feds prove it?"

"You personally."

"The feds sent down a file on him. With no fingerprints, we had to go off other things they had."

"Like what?"

"Tattoo on his chest."

"What was it of, if you don't mind me asking?"

"His last name. In case he forgot, I guess."

That makes me chuckle.

"Yeah," Vasquez says, "from what I've heard, the Giuseppe family tree wasn't exactly... blossoming... if you know what I mean."

I picture Antonio squeezing himself through the bathroom and accidentally dropping his bag of Burger King in the toilet.

And more recently, Goon with this extra bouncy Molotov. Although, to be fair, I have no idea if he is related.

"Yeah," I say, trying not to giggle again. "I dig."

"How this guy managed to avoid getting caught for so long seems like a miracle. I mean, I didn't know him, but from what I've heard through the grapevine... Yikes."

"Yeah, I heard they were going to bust him on a multi-level marketing scam."

Vasquez starts laughing now. "I heard that, too. I guess when you have enough money, you can get away with a lot of stuff. At least for a while."

"It always catches up to you, for sure. Were there any other things used to identify?"

"Yeah, he was wearing a ring. Some gaudy, one-of-a-kind thing that was his."

"It's stayed on his finger?"

"Yeah. It looked like it was tight to begin with, but that guy's hands swelled like Mickey Mouse's. The skin came off, but not that ring."

"There were no other signs of injury to the body?"

"Aside from the head wound that likely knocked him out before he drowned? No, I examined the entire body and did a full-body X-ray looking for internal injuries I may have missed. Water in the lungs and nothing in his stomach."

"Is that normal?"

"No food? Yeah. No. It all depends. It's hit or miss, so we rarely rely on stomach contents to tell us anything. Maybe if he had eaten right before he died, we could see what he ate, but if he had a granola bar in the morning and hadn't eaten lunch yet, it would be empty. Means nothing."

"Was there... a metal plate in his head?"

"A metal plate?"

"Yeah."

"No..." Vasquez says slowly. "Why?"

"No head injury other than the one that... you know, knocked him out?"

"No, nothing. Totally normal."

I'm quiet, trying to piece this all together.

"You there?" Vasquez asks.

"I'm here. Sorry. Thank you so much for your help. You called me on Castillo's phone – is she still there?"

"She's here."

"Can you put her on, please? Seriously, you've been a huge help. Huge!"

"Glad to. Hope I find out what this is all about soon."

"You will."

"Take care. Here's the sheriff."

"Hey," Castillo says. "What was that all about?"

"We need to figure it out and let you know. Were you able to run the names of people that worked at the Gazette when the two victims worked there?"

"Are you kidding me? You know how long that is going to take?"

Shit.

"Yeah, sorry. It was a long shot. Keep me posted?"

"You gonna tell me what that was all about with Vasquez?"

"Absolutely. Just not right now. I promise. One more favor. Pretty please."

Another loud sigh. "What?"

"The names of the two victims? From the paper, I mean."

"Google is your friend, Ms. Lemons. Call me back when you decide to not keep me in the dark about my own cases."

The call ends.

Yikes.

"What was that all about?" Archie asks.

"I got greedy. I tried to get as much information as I could. My bad."

"A valiant effort, my love."

"Well, at least one thing is for sure. Whoever that bloated corpse was, it wasn't Mongo. So who the hell was it? And where is Mongo now?"

"Well, it's clear that he faked his own death to get out of going to jail. That much is obvious now."

"His DNA was a near match to his sister, though, so this really makes no sense."

"It does. I just think we need to find out more about the brother that moved out west and these mysterious kids he has that nobody seems to know about. Something tells me one of them might be missing."

"Holy shit. You think Mongo killed his own brother or kids?!"

"My money is on the brother. Not only that, I think he had Antonio tattoo his chest and put a ring on his finger that was a little too snug."

"But... How did he pull this off? Everything just seemed so perfect."

"Yeah, a little too Raph."

174

"A little too Raph indeed. But what do we do? We have no idea where Mongo could be hiding. He could be in Cuba by now."

"I don't know. If he was able to flee, why not just flee? Why go through the trouble of faking your death. No, he's here somewhere, at least for now. Mark my words."

"Consider them marked. So how do we find him?"

"Huh? Oh, I don't know. I'm hungry."

"Come on. Focus. Let's put everything together and include Monica this time. I'm guessing Mongo got injured at one time, badly enough for surgery on his skull. It seems obvious that Monica was a part of that surgery and held on to those X-rays for whatever reason. Who knows? So when Mongo turns up dead on the beach, and there is no mention of a big metal plate in his head as an identifying mark, Monica makes a call."

"Do you think she was going to blackmail him?"

Sigh. "I don't know. It's possible. Or maybe she just knew it was bullshit and let them know. Or maybe they remembered her and contacted her. The other doctor is dead, so that leaves only one other person, that we know of outside of Mongo's circle, that can identify that body as not being him.

"I mean, I guess it doesn't matter what happened. Monica was almost murdered. Hell, she could very well be dead right now, and we just don't know it yet. I want these pieces of shit to pay."

"Well, two down," Archie says, his stomach growling.

"Well, I think the Goon is still alive."

"I was talking about Antonio and whoever that was that washed up on the beach." He puts the words *washed up* in air quotes. That body was definitely meant to be found.

ARCHiE

We're sitting on the patio of another beachside cafe waiting on our food. It's been a hell of a day, and I am dying to eat again. I swear to god, it feels like this day has been fifty hours long.

Elise is researching the two newspaper employees who were killed by Sam, trying to find their overlapping time at the job, while I'm enjoying the view of the ocean and moist air filling my lungs.

"I'm going to make a call," Elise says while holding her phone to her ear.

"I figured," I say, smiling.

"Hi," Elise says into the phone, "my name is Elise Lemons investigating the death of two of your former employees, Mr. Hector Bowen and Mr. Ian Goodman."

While Elise is on the phone, I make a call of my own.

"Max," I say.

"Hey buddy," Max says like the narwhal from *Elf*.

"Hey, so, I have another job for you."

"I haven't even finished the last one."

"Ditch it. Put it on the backburner. Doesn't matter right now."

He's eating something. I'm guessing something from a fast food place. I've never seen another human being shove more garbage in his mouth than Max. Even as a kid, it was nonstop. How he doesn't weigh five-hundred pounds, I'll never know.

With a full mouth, he says, "Whatcha need?"

"Frank Giuseppe, our gangster. He has a sister serving time up in New Jersey."

"Yep." *Chomp chomp chomp.*

"But he also has a brother that moved out west."

A rustle of papers and a cough, followed by, "Yep.

Vincent. Ol' Vinny Giuseppe didn't want anything to do with the family and moved out west to," he clears his throat, "start anew. He's off the radar, though. I did a little digging this morning. He's clean, as far as I can tell."

"He may be clean, but I'm pretty sure he's not alive."

"No shit?"

"No shit. I think the body that washed up on the shore was his, not Mongo's. I think Mongo lured his brother here and swapped places with him."

"Oh shit. So you think Mongo is out here?"

"I don't think so. At least not yet. He's lying low, waiting for the heat to be off before making a move. And when he does, I doubt it will be in the country."

"Good god, man. Adventure magnet, you are!"

"Yeah, I certainly appear to be, huh?"

"So, I'm confused. What do you need?"

"Just... try to see if you can find anything on him. Anything at all. See if he took a flight to Florida recently. Don't bother with commercial airlines. Even I don't think they would be that stupid."

"Charters?"

"Yeah... Possibly. Can you handle that?"

"Dude, my job is the most boring job you could possibly imagine. This... this is like Christmas morning 1988, unwrapping that glorious Nintendo, NES."

I fight the urge to correct him. It's either Nintendo, or NES. Not both. That would be Nintendo, Nintendo Entertainment System. See, makes no sense. Like PIN number.

I decide to let it slide. "Thanks, buddy. Call me ASAP."

"Can do!"

Elise is still on her phone. As soon as I drop mine back in my pocket, a woman in a sundress approaches, like she was just standing a few feet back waiting for me to finish my call. I was hoping she had my sandwich, but no dice.

"Yeah?" I say.

"Archie? Are you Archie Lemons, I mean?"

"I am."

Elise is paying zero attention to this attractive woman talking to me.

"My name is Annie. Um, Annie Jones."

"Is that your real name, Annie Jones?"

She giggles. "Yeah. Not very original, right?"

A Smith and a Jones in the same week, two Monicas and two Reynolds.

"It's cool. I dig it. So what's up, Annie Jones."

I'm trying to be friendly, but in reality, I am terrified of unwanted and spontaneous conversation. It's the main reason I avoid drive-thrus with overly friendly teenage employees.

"Um. I saw you on TV, and obviously, I know who you are, and I can't believe you're here because I have a major problem."

Of course she does. I'll give her until my sandwich arrives.

"Okay?"

"It's my husband. Well, technically, it's my, um, ex-husband? Maybe?"

"Not sure I'm following."

"He was executed."

Well, this took a shocking turn. "Like, in jail?"

"Yeah. He was... um... not great."

"I bet," I say, despite Florida having the fourth highest execution rate in America. I mean, it's no Texas, not even close, but it's up there.

"Yeah," she says nervously, looking down at her flip-flops.

Elise finally notices and gives me a quizzical look. I shrug quickly while Annie still isn't looking.

"So, what's the problem?"

"He's back."

"I'm sorry? Your executed husband is back?"

"Yeah. You're going to think I'm crazy, and that's totally fine, but we used to hang out by this little river that led into the Wetlands, just outside of town. We

---

178

would go there all the time; we had a little bench and everything. Three days ago, I got a note delivered to my desk. Here."

She hands me a piece of paper she's had tucked in her palm this whole time. I unfold it and read it:

> **Time to die, bitch!**
> **I told you I was get you if**
> **you testified against me.**
> **Now I'm back and I'm**
> **not leaving without you're head!**

Well, whoever wrote it isn't a big fan of proofreading, I see. *I was get you! You are head.*

Good lord.

"He's the only person I ever testified against, so I know it's him."

Move to Florida, they said. It'll be great, they said. Goddamn.

"Please don't think I'm crazy. The day after I got that one, I got another one that specifically mentioned our spot. He told me to meet him there."

"I'm confused. Your *dead* husband wants *you* dead and told you to meet him in your old spot so he can, what, kill you?"

"Yes."

"So don't go. Problem solved."

"You don't believe me."

"Look, kid. There are no such things as ghosts. Who delivered the letter? The post office?"

"No, no. Jimmy from the car dealership where I work."

"What do you mean?"

"I answer phones at a car dealership. Jimmy is a salesman. He gave me the letters. Said someone slipped them under the door."

"He gave you both letters?"

She nods her head like a happy child.

The waitress drops off our food, and I want nothing

more than to ditch this poor girl and eat. "Annie," I say, "does Jimmy happen to know about this special spot?"

"Of course. Jimmy knows all that stuff. He always comes over to talk to me throughout the day."

"Mmhmm. Does he do anything else nice for you?"

"All the time. He brings me coffee and snacks and all sorts of stuff."

"Mmhmm. And Jimmy knows about the letters and the ghost, right?"

"Oh yes, and he believes me."

"I bet he does."

"Obviously, before the letters arrived, he knew you believed in ghosts, spirits from the great beyond, stuff like that. Yeah?"

"Yeah. I tell Jimmy everything."

Elise ends her call and says, "Honey, did Jimmy offer to go out to this spot with you to protect you from the ghost of your dead husband?"

Annie's face brightens up to the closest thing to a smile since she got here. "He did! How did you know?"

"Babe, Jimmy is trash. He wrote the letters to manipulate you into loving him like he loves you. Men are garbage. Jimmy is a prime example."

"What, no, not Jimmy. He's funny."

"Babe," Elise says. "Ghosts don't send letters. This isn't *Scooby-Doo*. Something way scarier sent those letters, and he is, most definitely, human. The scariest monsters always are. Please report Jimmy to your HR as soon as you get to work."

Annie stands there silently for what seems like a full minute before finally taking the hint, saying thank you, crying, then finally leaving me to my sandwich.

"Florida, man. Who knew?"

"Poor girl," Elise says with a sympathetic look on her face. "Glad I've got you, my non-trash, lover."

"Aw, you're the sweetest. That was some impressive listening while you were on the phone, too."

"That case wasn't exactly hard to crack. But check this out. I found out the two victims worked at the paper together from 1999 to 2007."

"Not bad. Good work."

"It gets better. They both held top jobs simultaneously from 2004 to 2007, when Hector Bowen left the company. The other guy, Ian Goodman, held a top position until the company started to fold and turned into online only."

"Impressive work."

"Thank you. So, now I'm thinking, if this is the ball we're going to run with, ignoring the other two victims for now at least, we should focus on someone with money who knew these two guys. The first choice would be to see if there were any damning articles written about someone who maybe wants revenge. That's good in theory, but neither of these two were writers. They were stuffed-shirt businessmen. This leads me to my next theory – We're looking for someone who worked with them.

"Their salaries were good, but nothing to the point that they could be paying out hundred thousand dollar paydays to terminal hitmen."

"Unless," I say, genuinely impressed with my gorgeous wife's gorgeous brain.

"In every movie about a newspaper, the owner is always a rich asshole. Now, if we look at the two owners of the paper during that overlapping time, now we might get somewhere."

"So we check out these two people?"

Elise holds out a single finger. "One. One is dead. The other one lives about forty-five minutes away."

"We have to drive back to Palm?"

"That's up to you."

"Oh my god, why didn't we do that when we were there?"

"Um, well, we didn't know about all this."

"Aren't you exhausted?"

"Of course I am. We've been going nonstop since before dawn. But I also want to catch some bad guys."

"We promised the boys..."

"I know. But it doesn't get dark until like 9 o'clock. We'll be back long before then. I promise."

"Are you going to tell your BFF Castillo?"

Elise laughs a little. "I would like to check things out first, ya know, just me and you, the way I like it."

"Well, when you put it like that..."

"So we can go? We can come right back, I promise, and figure out what to do with the Mongo situation."

"We need to find that metal-headed turd, ASAP!"

"We will."

"It can't really be that simple, can it?"

"You think that was simple?"

"You know what I mean."

"I think that was some damn fine detective work, myself."

She's right. I smile at her and say, "It *was* some damn fine detective work. Detective."

"Thank you," she says, smiling back at me. She's blushing but trying to hide it.

"Hey, ya know what?" I say, remembering that I grabbed Goon's phone and tossed it in the front pocket of Elise's purse. "Holy shit. Let me see your purse."

Elise slides it over to me, and I grab the phone.

"I totally forgot!"

"Do you know the passcode?"

I type in 6969 then show the unlocked screen to Elise. "As a matter of fact, I do. Our Mr. Goon was a pretty clever guy. No one would ever guess 6969 for a four-digit passcode."

"Isn't that your passcode?"

"Shh, don't tell everybody. Gawd."

"Oh, you're absolutely right. My apologies."

"That's more like it," I say, laughing. 6969 is my new passcode after the kids figured out my previous passcode 1234, in a not-too-clever nod to *Spaceballs*.

I wouldn't care about them knowing how to get into my phone if they didn't use it constantly to order themselves pizzas or Target delivery orders on my credit card.

———

182

Lousy thugs.

To Elise, I ask, "Do you mind driving to Palm while I play on my new phone here?"

"Absolutely!"

Much to Elise's horror, I shove the rest of my sandwich in my mouth and say, "Let's roll, babydoll!"

ELISE

He just shoved half a grilled veggie sandwich on crunchy ciabatta bread into his mouth. I've never seen anything like it. Not only did he manage to still breathe somehow, but he could still talk.

My mind is blown!

Endlessly talented, my husband is.

ARCHiE

In the car, I open Goon's text messages. No luck there. The dumb idiot had the common sense to delete them, especially while carrying it with him and, ya know, committing murder.

The second place I look is a little advanced for someone who throws plastic bottle explosives at Floridian storm windows. It's an old trick from back in the day when I'd take any case I could get, which included proving the whereabouts of suspicious spouses.

It was dirty work, but it paid the bills.

This trick can be used on any operating system, but since Goon has an iPhone like me, I tap the Settings button and scroll down to Privacy. From Privacy, I tap on Location Services and scroll down to the very bottom, to System Services. I tap that and scroll down to Significant Locations, tapping that as well.

The next screen shows the locations of every place you've spent more than a few minutes recently.

Several locations pop up, including one towards the very top that says Sunrise Cove General Hospital. This sends a chill up my spine. He was there, waiting to finish the job that Antonio failed to do. Elise's call for protection on Monica saved her life.

The Crest Motel is here. That's where ol' Antonio took the big forever snooze.

Friggin' Arby's is here. According to this, he ate there twenty-one times in the past month. That explains his size and, possibly, baldness.

The Wetlands are on here six times. Nothing good could be happening in the Wetlands, a marshy swampland a few miles inland from here which houses many hungry critters and insects I hope never to meet.

A body could go missing quite easily in a place like that.

Paradise Motel, a different motel from where all the action happened, has fourteen hits. I bet he was staying there.

"Anything?" Elise asks.

"Almost too much. We're going to have to pawn some of these places off on the local fuzz. There's no way we can cover all of them.

"Can we get Castillo to help?"

"Only if there are any spots in her jurisdiction. There might be. I won't know until I look up all these places on the map."

"Is there anything we can do in the car?"

"I can call Murray, see if he's slept it off yet."

"Something tells me Murray is still at Monica's apartment complex, probably asleep in his car. What about Gene?"

"Fine. I'll call Gene."

I dial the Sunrise Cove Sheriff's Department, and Gene answers on the second ring. I fill him in on everything, then ask him how our Goon is doing.

"Well, he's burnt to a crisp and in a whole lot of pain."

"Do you know his name yet?"

"He had a wallet but no ID. Whole lot of money, though. Cash. No credit cards."

"Maybe he's not as dumb as he looked." I second-guess myself while visions of that 2-liter bottle bouncing off the window dance in my head. I would laugh in any other situation, but I know that burn victims are no joke, no matter how big of an asshole they are.

"Yeah... Maybe," Gene says, totally, ridiculously, clueless about what is going on.

"Look," I say, "we have his phone. He gave us the password, and we're not law enforcement, so we searched it. Two things. It looks like you putting a deputy outside of Monica's door saved her life. That guy was lurking, and if not for you and your team, that girl

186

would be dead. So, thank you."

"Wow," Gene says in shock. "That's... wow. Alright. What's the second thing?"

"It appears that the guy who washed up on our shores isn't who everyone thinks he is."

I tell the poor overloaded Gene the entire story of Mongo not really being Mongo.

Gene is so overwhelmed his voice is trembling.

"So here's what we need. We have the names of some places that the burn victim visited. We have reason to believe Mongo could be hiding out in one of them. The motels seem unlikelier than some of these locations, but they're all worth checking. Can you round up some deputies and go look for this guy?"

"Are you... Are you serious? I've worked here three months and you want me to track down the mob?"

I shrug. I don't know why, seeing as I'm on the phone, but whatever.

"Get a pen and piece of paper. Take down the locations. If you want to go, go. If not, we'll figure something else out when we're back. I'm sure you've seen *Andy Griffith* and know how to do a manhunt."

"Andy who?"

"Oh, Gene... Just get a pencil, please."

"Got it."

I list off a few locations, the Paradise Motel being one of them, then tell him good luck. "We'll be in touch."

"Oh my god. Where do I even start?"

"Well, is the burned guy awake? Why don't you try asking him."

"He's... He's not awake."

"So wake him up. What's the problem?" I'm trying not to laugh.

"I can't... Seriously?"

"Kid, I can't tell ya how to do your job. How about you throw Murray in a pool and sober him up? Worth a shot."

"I don't even know where he is."

"He's at Monica's apartment complex, probably

asleep."

"W-What?"

"Gotta go! You'll be fine. K bye-ee!"

I end the call. I can picture poor Gene just standing there, mouth open, still holding the phone to his ear, unable to move.

Poor bastard.

"Not too much longer," Elise says. "Is he going to do it?"

"No idea. That dude is so far out of his league he's like every other basketball team playing the Dream Team in the '92 Olympics."

"I have no idea what that means."

I laugh. Only the most incredible sports team ever assembled, beat every team they played by an average of forty-four points, but okay. "He's ridiculously out of his league."

Elise takes an exit we've never taken before en-route to our mystery guest's house. "Almost there."

"What's this a-hole's name?"

"To be fair, we don't know if he's an a-hole. It's just a hunch that you're basing on-"

"Well, if he has money, he's probably an a-hole."

"Exactly. But, ya know, we have money..."

"Yeah, but we're not all *moneyey* about it. I want to buy a truck with a duct-taped dash, and you're opening a community theater to bring art to the people."

"Fair enough. His name is... Homer Garrity."

"His name is not Homer Garrity! That's the name Jimmy Olsen used when he pretended to be a private eye in that old *Superman* episode, you big liar!"

She's laughing. "I forgot his name. Sue me. Open my phone. I wrote it in the notes section.

I grab her phone and open the notes. "Does Lowell Harmon sound familiar?"

"Yeah! Lowell. How could I forget that?"

It only takes us another five minutes to reach our last off-ramp and less than five more to find his neighborhood. It's gated, so we circle around and wait for another car to come in, then hightail it behind them, real sneaky-like.

The car's GPS tells us to turn left in half a mile, and our destination will be on our right.

"You found his exact address?"

"I'm no amateur," Elise says. "Remember?"

"I never cease to be impressed by you."

ELiSE

Well, the neighborhood is massive, which fits well with the houses and the lots they sit on, but the main thing that sticks out about it is how well hidden it is. If you weren't looking for it, you'd drive right past the front gate and never even notice.

Lowell Harmon's house is located at the very back, the last street. Aside from it being stunning, it butts up to a massive cluster of trees, vines, and various other foliage, which seems almost endless.

The street is all his.

"Well, he certainly has money," Archie says, unimpressed.

I pull up to the curb and we both get out. "Remember," I say, "we're just doing routine questioning. We know nothing, and we suspect nothing."

"Yep. Got it."

"You sure? You've been known to... ya know... get irritated with people pretty quickly."

"Nope. This is Beach Mode Archie. Cool as a cucumber in a bowl of hot sauce, baby."

Before I can even knock on the door, it opens, revealing an older brunette woman in scrubs and thick glasses. "Sorry," she says, "I happened to see you walking up."

"Oh, um, it's okay. We were hoping to speak to Lowell Harmon."

"Well, you've come to the right place. We don't usually get visitors. May I tell him what this is about?"

"It's about the death of a few of his old co-workers."

"Oh dear."

"I'm sorry," Archie says, "who are you?"

"I'm his nurse, Rosalie Nunez."

"Oh," I say. "Is he ill?"

"No, I just come by to check on him. He's..." She lowers her voice, "getting up there in years, so I come by a few times a week to check on him."

"How long have you been doing that?"

"Going on four years now."

"Long time for someone who isn't sick," Archie says, already getting that tone I was worried about.

"Well, the pay is good and I like to think I help."

"Of course you do," I say. "So, do you mind if we have a few words with him? We'll try not to upset him. We're just trying to help solve these cases and, honestly, we need all the help we can get."

"Are you with the... sheriff's department?"

"Yeah," Archie says, lying. I can't help but think of the Florida Man who used the plastic badge and said 'I the police.'

I try not to giggle.

Before she asks to see our badge, thus making us look like idiots, I quickly say, "We're consultants. We have to do the work the sheriff's don't have time for. Like driving all over and talking to everyone that knew any of these victims."

"Oh, Uncle Sam's victims? I've been following along on the news. It's like a bad horror movie."

"I mean," Archie says rather aggressively, "there really are no bad horror movies. Even the less-than-stellar ones have their merits, ya know. Let's not get crazy here."

If I could face-palm myself right now, I totally would.

Rosalie looks at him like his hair is on fire.

"Sorry," I say, "can we just please talk to him."

After a few more moments of staring, Rosalie says, "Of course. Please come in."

We take a few steps inside and wait in the middle of a massive foyer. It's even bigger than how it appears from the outside. Above us, a chandelier sways with the breeze from the open door. Rosalie leaves the room and loudly says, "Lowell. You have some visitors."

"Hell of a view," I say, peering out the massive front windows out onto the ocean.

Archie shrugs. "Eh. I like our house better."

This makes me smile. "You know what, me too."

"Psh, who has a chandelier at the beach? Get real."

"Do I know you?"

Lowell Harmon is walking into the room wearing a plush robe and possibly nothing else. Archie cringes then tries to play it off like he didn't... badly.

"No," I say. "My name is Elise Lemons. This is my husband, Archie. We're making the rounds of anyone and everyone who knew any of the victims of the..."

"Uncle Sam?"

"Yes."

"I've been following the story, though not too closely. So much bad news these days, I prefer watching QVC."

This causes my husband to smile and nod like he and Lowell are long-lost best friends. During quarantine, Archie developed a rather unhealthy obsession with watching QVC.

"I feel you," Archie says, bumping the side of his fist to his heart two times then pointing to Lowell.

Oh my god.

"So," Lowell says, "you've certainly done your homework if you tracked me down. I haven't worked in over a decade, and with either of those two guys longer than that."

"Yeah, I know. Like I said, we're the ones that have to do all the boring routine work. But, you know what they say, no stone left unturned."

"Understandable. Would you like to come sit down?"

"That won't be necessary unless you are uncomfortable."

"I'm fine."

I must say, Lowell isn't as old as I was expecting, especially when a nurse answered his door. He seems like a perfectly healthy man of about seventy - No cane, no limp, no liver spots, no saggy balls dangling below his robe... just a normal guy.

God, sorry, that was gross. I've been hanging around Archie and a bunch of pre-teen boys for way too long.

"So, I mean, we have to ask, did you know either of the other two victims? The ones you didn't work with?"

Lowell laughs, "Of course not."

I smile. "Didn't think so."

"Did you have a feud with either of the two victims you did know?"

"My dear, I'm too old for feuds. Even if I did have one back in my working days, that's so far in the past, it's not even worth remembering. I've done quite well for myself, as you can see. I have no need for... feuds." He says that last part with disgust.

"Do you own a gun?" Archie asks bluntly.

"Heavens no. We have our own private security here. I'm quite safe. It does puzzle me, however, how you got in here."

"Piggybacked," Archie says flatly. "Guard was out. So no gun?"

"Of course not. You can't possibly think I did this, right?" He laughs, "I mean, that's preposterous. I was sitting right in there when that fella was shot the other day. I got the alert on my phone, and Rosalie turned the local news on."

How convenient. "What days does she come, Mr. Harmon?"

"Oh, she is here every other day, sometimes more if I need her. I pay her quite well, so she should have no real qualms about it."

"I'm sure she doesn't."

"Are we done here? Your questions bore me. I'm sorry those gentlemen were all shot, but like I said, it wasn't me. I have no grudges, and I certainly have no reason to kill. Absurd. Absolutely absurd." He turns to return to wherever he came from. "Rosalie, show our guests out."

Rosalie appears, seemingly out of nowhere, and says, "Of course."

When Lowell is out of the room, Rosalie walks us outside and closes the door to just a crack behind her. "Please excuse him. He's just tired."

"It's fine."

Rosalie closes the door completely and whispers, "I do need to tell you something, though. He does own a gun. He got it about a year ago after there was a robbery in the neighborhood."

"Where is it?" Archie asks.

"That's the thing. It's been gone for about a year, too. He was real gung-ho about it for a few weeks – he'd go out into the backyard and open fire on the trees. He'd say he'd like to see any burglar try to get into his house. He must have shot five boxes of bullets into those trees before I caught him spinning it on his finger, like some cowboy in those movies he watches. I insisted he put that damn thing away... So he did. Gone. Completely forgotten about ever since that day. I have no idea where he got it or where he put it, but I never saw it again, and I doubt he has, either."

"So what does that mean?"

"Mr. Harmon seems fine on the outside, but sometimes his memory slips a bit and he forgets things that he should remember. Now, I'm only telling you this because I don't want you to check if he owns a gun and you find out and think he's lying. He's not. He just forgot. It could be anywhere. But, one thing I can promise you is that he did not shoot those men. I can vouch for him."

"I'm sure you can, Rosalie. I have no doubt that he didn't shoot them," I say, smiling.

"Okay, good." Rosalie wipes pretend sweat from her brow and says, "Phew."

"He's able to get around okay, though?" Archie asks. "Like, he can drive a car? He looked pretty good for his age. My dad is sixty-eight and can't do anything. That's why I ask."

Archie's dad has been dead for a decade.

"Oh yes," Rosalie says. "He's fully capable. I just

help him out. Plus, I think he likes the company."

"Thank you for your time," I say, ending the conversation.

"Of course. Hope all this helps."

In the car, Archie says, "I think you cracked this case. I don't trust that son of a bitch at all."

"Neither do I. You really think I cracked it?"

"I do. I'm proud of you. You figured this out by using logic and deductive reasoning instead of outright clues. That's not easy to do. But there is still a massive problem. There is no way we can prove this, you know. That asshole probably has a safe filled with bills and briefcases. And the gun could be anywhere. Hell, the next guy could already have it."

I sigh. "I know." Shit. "I know."

"We have to go home. Poor Jamie is probably bald by now and teetering on the brink of insanity."

"Yeah. Poor James. Let's go."

We pull out of the fancy neighborhood and get back onto A1A North, headed home.

ARCHiE

Jamie hadn't ripped all her hair out when we got home. In fact, she seemed totally fine. Brioni was just leaving when we got back, but Aryam, Eric, Milo, and Elliot were still in the backyard. Gary was assed-out flat on his back in his Pack n Play.

"Finally," Elliot yells when he sees we're back. "God! We have to go get fireworks! All the good ones are gonna be gone!"

"We passed seven hundred stands in the last mile. We'll be fine, buddy."

I'm exhausted and want nothing more than to plop on the sofa and fall asleep. But Elliot's right. I did promise we'd go.

Elise says she's going to stay with Gary and Jamie, and we can go without her. This makes absolutely no difference to the kids, who are storming out the front door with the pure ecstasy of kids getting to buy miniature explosives.

"We'll be back," I say as Elise falls on the sofa next to Jamie.

"Have fun."

"Yeah," Jamie says, "have fun. Get me something loud."

"Can do."

"We need to pick up Brioni and her sister," Elliot yells.

"Dude, she just left."

"Duh. She went home to get money."

"Obviously."

"And her sister. Remember?"

"Yes, Elliot. I remember."

"So can we go get her?"

"Dude, she lives fifty yards away. We can go get

her."

"Okay, sweet!"

Those damn kids cost me three hundred dollars at the firework stand. Absolutely incredible. What audacity. Get a job!

At least Brioni tried to pay for her own. I told her to keep the money, and just tell her mom that she used it. That made her giggle and she agreed to the scheme, but I knew there was no way she would stick to it. She's too honest.

Unlike the group of thugs she hangs out with.

As for the fireworks, the kids must have touched every single item the stand had for sale, making sure to get only the best, and loudest, ones.

One is called Screamin' Meemie, and I'm pretty sure its only goal is to cause tinnitus. They also look strikingly similar to the fireworks the shirtless idiots were pounding with a hammer and wrapping in duct tape to make their cherry bombs.

Makes me feel really safe, let me tell ya.

When we finally make it back home, Aryam's parents are waiting for us at the curb. Aryam must have texted them and said we were running a bit late. No big deal.

She says her goodbye, hugging everyone, myself included, then gets in the backseat, saying she'd see us in a week or so. I bullshit with her dad for a few minutes, then they take off.

I can see how sad Eric is to see her leave.

Adorable.

I'm bummed she won't be able to be here for the big fireworks show, but she has her own thing to do, I suppose. I made sure she was loaded up with explosives before she left. Hopefully, she'll have a good time with them and not lose any fingers.

Inside, I'm finally able to plop down in my chair. Elise is sprawled out on the sofa with her head nestled on Jamie's lap. She's fast asleep.

Jamie whispers, "I've had to pee for an hour."

I smile and tell her to get up and go, I'll take care of Elise's head.

Jamie scoots out from under Elise as I take support of my wife's head in my hands. Jamie runs to the bathroom, and when she returns, she scoots back in and I return Elise to her original position. She never knew.

To Jamie, I say, "Want to stay for a movie?"

"You don't mind?"

"Not at all. You can even pick."

"Oh," Jamie says. "I don't care. Eric, why don't you pick?"

His smile has returned. "Okay!"

He picks one of my favorite recent movies, *Ready or Not*. If you haven't seen it yet, check it out. I'd like to think Eric picked it for my benefit, but I think it has more to do with the leading lady having more than a passable resemblance to Jamie.

In a shocking twist of events, literally everyone is asleep before I am. I can't say I blame them. Today was a hell of a day.

ELiSE

"Happy Fourth of July!"

This is how Elliot wakes us up, by barging into our room and shouting.

Still groggy, I ask, "What time is it, dude?"

"Noon!"

This gets my attention and I sit up in bed, shocked by how late I slept in. "Noon?!"

"Yep! Don't worry, Gary has had breakfast but he probably wants lunch now. Possibly someone else wants lunch as well."

"Would that be you, Elliot?"

"It's possible!"

"Thank you for feeding your brother, honey."

"No sweat!"

"What is going on here?" Archie asks, his face buried in his pillow.

"It's noon."

"So?"

"That's late. We have stuff to do."

"I don't wanna."

"Yesterday was brutal. I'm on vacation."

"You can't be on vacation."

"Then I'm on strike."

Forty-five minutes later, Archie is conscious and in the living room being harassed by the boys about the fireworks.

"We can't do them in daylight," Archie says. He's so annoyed. I love it. "What kind of psychopath lights fireworks in the daytime?"

"Those guys from the motel parking lot," Eric says with some snark.

"Yeah, and we all saw what happened there. Now

quit bothering me or you're getting mayonnaise for dinner."

After the kids are fed, Archie and I sit at the table, deciding what we should do. We're sixty-five to seventy-five percent sure Lowell Harmon is our man but have absolutely no way to prove it.

We could pass it off to Castillo; have her get a search warrant, and turn that place upside down. But again, I don't think she would find anything. On top of that, us showing up there tipped him off. All he has to do now is stop, ditch the gun and costume, and he gets away scot-free.

Ugh, why did I stick my nose in on this case? I'm like some random bored mom on Facebook that butts into other people's arguments in comment sections then plays the victim when she's torn to shreds.

That's me now.

I'm no better.

I may as well just cut an A-line in my hair and put on some capri pants, because I'm her now.

Ugh.

I did call Gene first thing this morning, though, or should I say, afternoon, and despite him actually doing the legwork, came up empty. I have to hand it to the kid; he really came through. I mean, he didn't find anything, but he saved us a lot of time.

Monica is still out cold. It's a fifty-fifty shot she'll survive. *She'll either come out of it, or she won't.* That's what they told Gene, at least.

It doesn't exactly fill me with sunshine and rainbows.

It's a holiday, so I don't know how productive today will be. I feel like I'm stuck. This time a week ago, I could hardly wait for today, but now I just feel... numb.

And exhausted.

I tip back in my chair, put my hands behind my head, running my fingers through my hair, and sigh. "This sucks."

"Well," Archie says, "I mean, we figured everything out. For two people who just got to town, with no licenses, no authority, and no real clue about the state, we did pretty well."

"Pretty well doesn't cut it without the proof. Whatever is keeping Mongo here isn't going to keep him forever, and if he leaves, that's that. It's over." I laugh. "Hell, we don't actually know if he's still here. We're just guessing."

"Yeah, but it's a guess based on facts. And a good guess. He's officially dead now. He's not just boarding a plane to Paraguay. He's stuck. He knows it. At least until the heat is off from the dumb feds."

"He could have taken a boat."

"Sure. To where? Cuba? Puerto Rico? Then what? Plus, they found his boat abandoned, remember? That's what started this whole mess."

Another sigh. "Yeah, I guess." I put my chair back on all-fours and lean forward on the table. "I just wish-" Something catches my eye in the living room.

"You just wish what?"

Holy shit.

"Um. Elise?"

"I've got to call Castillo and have her get a warrant for Lowell's place."

"It's a holiday. That's not going to happen."

I ignore him. "Grab the kids. Road trip!"

"What? Seriously? You want to be on the roads... in Florida... on the biggest drunk holiday of the year?"

"We'll be fine. Get the kids."

"I'm so sick of driving," Archie whines, but I ignore him.

While dropping Gary off at Liz and Our Monica's house and getting their permission for Milo to come with us, we picked up Jamie, who was out front watering her flowers and wanted to come. I'm sure that pleased Eric.

When I called Castillo, she told me she would do her best to get the warrant. The judges in Palm Beach, she said, were pretty good about granting them. She said it shouldn't be a problem if it pertains to Uncle Sam.

I laid out the proof we had, and while it was flimsy, it was promising. Especially if we could get the evidence I'm hoping we can.

When we pull into Lowell's neighborhood, Castillo is there waiting for us. She's already talked to the man working the front gate, so it was open. Archie and I hopped out of our car and handed over driving duties to Jamie, giving her instructions on exactly where to go.

We got into Castillo's SUV and rode the rest of the way up. When we turned on Lowell's street, Jamie continued on straight to the dead-end.

"You guys sure about this?" Castillo asks before we step out of the car.

Archie shrugs. "Yeah, maybe. Better than nothin', right?"

"Well," she says, "here goes nothing."

We get out of the car and head up to the door. Rosalie isn't there to open it for us this time, so Castillo knocks. And by knocks, I mean she's acting like the door was a grown man that was dating her underage daughter. She's wailing on that thing like she's Cobra Kai.

Lowell throws the door open with fury, obviously pissed by this interruption. "What?!" he yells before recognizing us. "Oh god damn it, you again?'

I wave, smile, and say, "Me again. Miss us, Cutie-pie?"

"No."

"That's too bad," Archie says. "We sure missed you."

"What is this about?" Lowell asks Sheriff Castillo. "They conned you into coming out here?"

"No con," I say. "By the way, this is Sheriff Castillo, in case you were wondering."

"I wasn't. "

"Well, it's still polite to do introductions."

"What do you want? I'm busy."

Castillo says, "It's been brought to my attention, Mr.

Harmon, that you have a connection to two of the victims."

Lowell laughs and says, "So what? You drove out here twice because I knew two of the victims a hundred years ago?"

"Not quite a hundred years, but yeah."

"Poppycock!"

I've never heard someone say that in real life. It's pretty funny.

"Well," Castillo says, "it might be *poppycock*, but, ya know, we're here anyway. Ever been to First Street Baptist Church?"

"I don't know what that is."

'That's weird. Ever heard of a man named Carl Benson?"

"Nope."

"How about Peter Eastman?"

"No," Lowell says, quieter this time. I'm now one-hundred percent sure we've got the right guy.

"That's weird, too," Castillo said. "He got shot in the belly and bled out, right there in the church parking lot. You didn't hear about that?"

"Guess I missed that bit of news."

"You own a gun, sir?"

"No."

"We ran your name and it came back that you didn't, but the weird thing is, we have it on good authority that you did. At least at one time. I can't help but wonder where it went. And, since it's not registered in your name, where it came from."

"Crazy, right?" I say.

"Alright, Pops," Archie says, "how about you just confess to being behind the Uncle Sam killings, and my wife and I can get back home in time to light our street on fire."

"If you have a problem with me, Tubby, you can speak to my lawyer. In the meantime, how about you, your skinny slut wife, and your pet pig, get the hell off my property before I call security."

Archie is smiling - wide and glorious. He's so happy. His wife just got called a slut, and he got called fat, but he is glowing. Absolutely beaming, in fact. Pure, unbridled happiness.

Because, from a block away, Elliot is yelling, "We got it! We got it!"

Here they come!

Rounding the corner and headed straight for us are the boys, so excited they're jumping and spinning while running. Milo, triumphantly holding his metal detector in the air, yells, "I'm Columbo!"

I lock eyes with Jamie. She smiles and nods.

We got him

"What the hell is this all about?!" Lowell yells at us. "Who are these people? I'm calling security."

"Did you forget that I'm the sheriff, sir? I think I overrule private security."

The boys arrive and drop four bullets into Archie's hand. "Well, looky here," he says. "Bullets."

"What?" Lowell says. "So what?"

"Don't you get it?" I ask. "These bullets came from the trees behind your house. Your nurse let it slip that you did, in fact, own a gun, and fired several practice rounds in your backyard. We sent my boys back there to find them."

"Nonsense!" Lowell barks. "You have... You have no right to be on my property! I'll have you all arrested for trespassing!"

Castillo interrupts him by calmly unfolding her warrant and holding it directly in front of his face. "You haven't met all my newest deputies, have you?"

The boys are making a ruckus.

"Now," Castillo says, "all we need is to match these. Give me a second." She presses the button on her radio pinned to her uniform and says, "Come on up." To Lowell, she says, "You're not going to want to miss this. I have a feeling this is going to be one explosive Independence Day."

"And ironic," Archie adds sarcastically. When

nobody responds, he clarifies, "Because he... ya know, won't have independence."

Thud.

Half a minute later the forensics van turns the corner and parks behind Castillo's SUV. Castillo holds up the pointer finger on both her hands and tells Lowell to sit tight for just one minute. "It won't take long. Why don't you come with me? We can all watch."

We follow her down to the curb, and Archie hands the bullets over to the same lab guy we met previously. "Why am I not surprised," he says when he sees us.

I just smile.

"This is ludicrous! You have no proof those came from my backyard!"

"Boys," Archie says, "were there more back there?"

"Tons!" Milo says.

"We had to dig these out of the tree with a knife," Jamie says, "but yeah. That metal detector was ringing like crazy."

I look at Lowell and give him a *too bad* shrug.

He looks like he's going to explode, like the top of his head will pop off and sparks will come shooting out.

Seems fitting for today.

It almost makes it funny.

"It's a match," the lab tech says.

In an instant, Castillo went from lighthearted to hardboiled. She grabs Lowell by the arms and pushes him against the side of the van... hard. "You son of a bitch!"

With zero interest in Lowell's comfort, she twists his arms back and cuffs him.

"That's too tight," Lowell gasps. "It's too tight!"

"Call security," Castillo says sarcastically, pulling him back and practically dragging him to her SUV. "You killed five people in my peaceful beach town, you son of a bitch. You're never going to see the light of day again. Why?"

"Yeah, Lowell," Archie says. "Why?"

Lowell is silent for a moment. He purses his lips

---

together tightly, deciding whether or not to tell us anything. Eventually, he says, "I was being blackmailed. But..."

"You didn't know by who," I say.

He nods. "I didn't know who."

"What did they have on you?" Castillo asks in the un-friendliest manner possible.

Lowell shakes his head. "No. Doesn't matter. It was someone at the paper; that much is obvious. I had to pay that son of a bitch twenty-five thousand dollars a month for years and I was fed up. I figured if I killed one suspect a month and one random, it wouldn't draw as much suspicion, and when the demands stopped, I would know who it was, and I would stop."

"So you killed innocent people?!" Castillo practically yells.

"Oh no, my dear. They were all guilty of something, just not of blackmailing me. I did my research. Nobody on the up and up would have been harmed. I can promise you that much."

"That means nothing to me. You had no right!"

Lowell shrugs.

I could point out that the people who worked at the paper were pretty innocent, since they weren't the ones blackmailing him, but I just keep my mouth shut and let the sheriff have this one.

Castillo slams the door in his face and looks at us. "Incredible."

The kids are still cheering, jumping up and down, ya know, being typical kids after catching a mass murderer. "Best Fourth of July ever," Milo yells, high-fiving all of us, one after another, even Castillo, who seems to be in a much better mood now.

To us, she says, "Guess I was wrong about you two. Great work." She reaches out her hand for Archie to shake, then me.

"You have our number," I say. "Use it any time."

"I might take you up on that. Again... truly... thank you."

ARCHiE

It turns out we had it almost entirely right. Lowell pulled a Tyler Durden and was invading terminal support groups, listening to them talk, figuring out which ones had lost faith or didn't believe in the afterlife, ones that didn't fear punishment after death. He approached them, exploited their disease with the promise of making their families better off after they passed.

Truly disgusting.

The guy who was shot in his car... Well, he didn't go for it. Lowell approached him and conned his way into the car with the promise of who knows what. Our dead man said no, so he had to be exterminated.

Lowell claims it was an accident. That the man tried to grab the gun from him, and there was a struggle. It really doesn't matter either way.

He also claims he didn't know the names of the other terminal men he used, but it didn't matter. The news would break, and the recipients of his blood money will figure it out. What they choose to do with it is none of my business, so who gives a shit?

I feel bad about Sarah, though. She'll probably lose her money, but something tells me she wouldn't have kept it anyway.

We're just getting back on to A1A to go home and celebrate our country's independence when I press my luck with Carl Benson's truck one more time. "Ya know," I say, "I could buy that truck and pay her... ya know... a little more than it's worth."

Elise smiles and rolls her head on the headrest towards me. "How much more?"

"I'm sure we can come to an agreement."

"Why do you even want that thing?"

"I just do."

We drive on for another mile or so, the kids having a party in the back, poor Jamie trapped in the middle. After another mile or so, Elise says, "You can get it. If you really want it."

"I do. Thanks."

"Oh please, I'm not your boss. You were going to buy it anyway."

We both laugh.

"Ya know," Elise says, "we still have some time before the sun goes down and the fireworks start."

"I'm pretty sure the boys brought them, just in case."

"Oh," Elise says, "they totally did. I'm surprised Elliot didn't try to sneak Brioni in the back of the car."

"Ha. Yeah."

"So, I was thinkin'."

"Uh oh."

"The Wetlands had several hits on Goon's GPS... and the turnoff is coming up..."

"You want to drive through the Wetlands?"

Elise twists in her seat, fully facing me now, looking extra adorable because she knows how much of a pushover I am for her. "I mean, we can just cruise through. His phone is in my purse. Fully charged..."

"Oh, it's fully charged?"

Elise giggles and says, "Maybe I had the foresight to plug it in this morning. You know, just in case."

"We have the kids. And Jamie."

"I just said go for a drive. That's all."

"But the Wetlands? They have bugs out there the size of feet."

"Don't even have to get out. Just a quick detour."

"Fine. Guys, you okay with a quick detour? We'll still be home in time for the festivities."

"Okay!" one of them yells. I'm not even sure which one.

To Elise, I ask, "Can you even drive out there?"

She shrugs. "Only one way to find out."

The Florida Wetlands is a massive clump of swamp and marshland that starts in the very south of the state and works its way up inland before eventually just ending where industry has taken over. The spot marked on Goon's GPS is towards the northern tip, hence why it's, according to Elise, *on our way home.*

When we get there, upon seeing it, the best way to describe it is if you've ever seen any movie set in the bayous of New Orleans, it's like that. Hell, if you've ever been on Pirates of the Caribbean at Disneyland, before the first drop, that's what this looks like.

I can literally hear the bugs outside my rolled-up window. The paved road ended about a quarter mile back. Now we're some weird dirt and rock mixture. There are definite tracks out here, though, and the farther we drive, the darker it gets, both from the massive Cyprus cover and, ya know, because it's getting later.

According to the phone, we're on the right track, but I don't think I want to go much farther. Especially with the kids. I'm just about to bring this to Elise's attention when she says, "Holy shit. Stop the car."

"What?" Before my foot is entirely down on the break, all three boys poke their heads through the front seats, right between us.

"What's going on?" Eric asks.

"Up ahead," Elise says. "There's a house."

She's right. It's way up there, but it's there. Calling it a house would be overselling it a bit. It looks more like a shack that's about to fall into the water.

"I'm going to call Gene," Elise says. "While I still have a signal."

ELiSE

"Gene, is Sheriff Murray awake?"

"Ms. Lemons?"

"Yeah. Is Murray awake?"

"Yeah, he's awake."

"Good. What kind of phone do you have?"

"Um, iPhone?"

"Is this your private number or the office number?"

"Um. Office?"

"Give me your private number. The iPhone number."

"Really?"

"Yes, Gene! Give me your number." He does. "I'm going to send you a location. I need you to grab Murray and whoever else is close and get here as soon as possible. Like, leave right now. You better drive, though."

I give him a few more details and end the call. He told us to observe and report. I agreed. I just didn't tell him I would be observing from much closer.

I open the car door and step out.

"You're not seriously going out there," Jamie says, shocked.

"Have to," I say, leaning back in and popping the glove compartment. I pull out the lockbox I keep inside, type in the code so no one can see, then pull out my gun. I hate this goddamn thing, but sometimes it's good to have in situations like this.

I grab the handcuffs, too.

"Really?" Archie says, his shoulders slumped. "We can't handcuff anyone here. We're normal citizens."

"Just in case. Calm down." I throw them on his lap. "Can you carry those for me?"

Archie realizes it's pointless to try and talk me out of this. He opens the door and slowly steps out onto the damp land below. "Man, these shoes are new."

"I'll buy you new ones, babe, I promise."

"Sure. Brand new Superstar Americanas... you'll just buy me some new ones. Sure, Elise. Sure. Ugh. First blood, now this."

"I know, I know. I'm sorry."

"Gah!" Archie yells while swatting at some unseen bug.

"Shh. Guys," I say to the boys, "be on the lookout. If you see anything we should be worried about, you honk this horn and we'll come running. Cover all directions. That means one of you looking out each way. James, you okay?"

"Never thought I'd lead such an exciting life. My goodness. Please be careful. Who knows what's up there, and there could be alligators and... It's so dark. Do you have to go?"

"That poor girl is in the hospital barely clinging to life."

I don't need to say anything more. Jamie gets it.

"Keep the car running. We'll be back. Love you."

"Love you, too," Jamie says. The boys didn't even hear me. They're already in their positions.

I close the door quietly and take a few steps to the front of the car where Archie is. You should see the look on his face. Classic.

"You know when you're walking in the backyard," he says, "and you step in a pile of dog crap? That's what every step feels like here."

"You ready?"

"Are you regretting that decision?" he asks, nodding towards me. My dress. It's a little short.

"It's a holiday at the beach. I just wanted to dress cute. I didn't know we'd end up in the marshes of hell."

"Yes you did!"

"You're wearing shorts. Bugs can just as easily fly up your legs as they can mine."

"This is pure torture. I hope you know that."

"I know. Come on. Let's go."

"It's dark as shit back – Gah, what was that?"

"Something splashed in the water."

"Oh great. I'm going to get eaten by an alligator."

"You're not going to get eaten. I have my gun. Worst case scenario is a bite on the leg." I laugh. "Now come on."

We take off walking, the ground so damp and sticky it's like walking across glue. Fifty yards from the house, things become clearer.

It's a shack, definitely, two rooms, maybe, with a covered patio area that looks like it might actually be sticking out over the water. Another thing notable about this crap-shack is that it looks like it's leaning. Like, the whole building could just fall at any moment. The boys would have it collapsed in less than a minute.

"You okay?" I ask a clearly struggling Archie.

"These bugs, man. Give me your gun."

"You can't shoot bugs, dork."

"It wasn't the bugs I was going to shoot. I've had a good run. This is it. Come on, hand it over."

"Oh, stop. Hold on."

Movement in the shack. A light just flicked on.

We stop in our tracks and take cover behind a tree. "Shit."

"What?"

"Don't move," I say as an alligator cuts across the dirt road fifteen feet ahead of us. Shooting an animal is the last thing I want to do, but it's better than being attacked. My gun is gripped tightly in my right hand as we both watch the dinosaur-like creature make it to the water and slide in.

"Phew."

"Come on."

There is a dumpster at the rear of the shack that is almost overflowing. Not a lot of trash collection out in these parts, I imagine. It's a good place to take cover, so we carefully make our way up to it. It smells worse than the water.

From inside, a man's booming voice echoes. "What

the hell do you mean?! I'm dying out here!"

The biggest shock I've had in a very long time comes when I turn and see Archie digging through the dumpster. Now here is something I never thought I'd see. The lid is up, and he is rummaging through it. What he's looking for is anybody's guess.

The man from inside is still yelling, and it's quite frightening. Add to that; I just saw a couple of red eyes off in the distance staring at us. Whatever the hell that is, I hope I don't find out.

Maybe this wasn't the best idea. "Let's get the hell out of here," I whisper. "The cops can handle this."

Some branches snap behind us, causing me to jump. Another alligator. So much for that idea.

Shit.

This one isn't minding his business. He's coming right for us.

"Shit, Archie, jump!"

He sees the danger and hops up on the corner of the dumpster. I take the other corner and pull my legs up. The alligator is directly below us, glaring.

"Look," Archie says, seemingly ignoring the immediate danger three feet below us.

"What?"

He pulls out a large bag from the trash.

"What the hell is that?" I whisper.

"It used to be a twenty pound bag of rock salt."

"So?"

"You know what happens if you dump this in a bathtub filled with fresh water and hold your brother's head under it? He drowns in the ocean."

"Holy shit. So we've got him. This is it."

"I would say so, yes."

Reminding us that we're still in very real danger, the alligator growls, seriously growls, then bashes his head into the front of the dumpster. The blow is so powerful we both almost fall into the rancid trash. I was not expecting that.

"Holy shit," Archie whisper-yells. "Are you okay?"

The alligator backs up and charges again, this time succeeding in knocking us both into the disgusting trash. Archie must be in absolute hell, but even worse, I dropped my gun. It's here somewhere. "I'm okay. Shit."

"What?"

"Gun."

The alligator launches another attack, this one so powerful the dumpster rocks backward a bit. This is bad... and about to get much worse. I hear the screen door on the shack slam shut. Archie and I both freeze, trying desperately not to make a sound.

We can hear the alligator charging and brace ourselves for impact - but it never comes. What follows is even more terrifying.

Gunshots

The echo inside the metal dumpster is almost deafening.

Still, we remain quiet.

I have begun *seriously* rethinking my decision to come out here.

Shit.

ARCHiE

"What the hell is going on here?!" Mongo yells before turning the corner. Elise and I do our best to hide in the dumpster, but it's pathetic at best. For now, at least, he doesn't seem to see us. His attention is focused on the alligator. He aims his gun at the creature and fires a shot into its side. It scampers away as best it can. It doesn't have much longer to live, and if we get out of this, I'll do my best to make sure it doesn't suffer... as awful as that sounds.

The gunshots caused an awful lot of noise aside from the obvious. Tons of hidden birds and creatures are scurrying into the great unknown. It's weird to think all these guys were around us and we had no idea.

Elise, apparently braver than I wish to be at the moment, yells, "Drop it, Mongo. Game over."

"What the-" He's about to draw his gun on us but thinks better of it when he sees Elise's pointed straight at him.

"Who the hell are you?!

"I'm Elise. This is Archie. Hi." She lifts her leg out of the dumpster and hoists herself out, the gun never leaving Mongo's face.

I go next.

"Hell of a plan, though," I say. "No qualms about killing your brother?"

"How... How'd you know that?"

Elise taps her left forefinger to the side of her head and says, "We're smart."

"Not that smart."

Behind us, the undeniable sound of a shotgun being pumped.

Shit.

I turn slowly and see a naked woman with a towel

wrapped around her holding us in her sights. "That's my wife, Brandy," Mongo says. "I'd love for you to meet her."

"Didn't even know you were married?"

"Well," Mongo says, "not yet. She used to be my brother's wife up until a little bit ago. Ain't that right, Sugar Tits?"

"That's right, baby."

"Well..." I say, my heart pounding so hard I can feel it in my brain. "How about we take off, and you guys get back to whatever it was you were doing. Ya know, come to think of it, I don't remember why we even came out here."

"So," Elise says, "you killed your own brother and planted him at the beach... for what?"

"Listen broad. I've avoided prison for sixty years; I'm sure as shit not goin' now. Especially not for peddling some bullshit product to bored white women. My brother was an asshole. Left the family behind years ago to work at a grocery store. Don't you think that stone-cold fox there deserves a little better than that?"

Stone-cold fox wouldn't be the words I used to describe the woman currently pointing her shotgun at us. To me, she looks like raw pork chops and Chiclets, but hey, beauty is in the eye of the beholder.

"So what? You guys lured him out here and drowned him in the bathtub."

Mongo laughs. "Let the son of a bitch soak for so long his skin was falling off."

"And everything was going great until your old nurse showed up."

"Bitch. Threatened to ruin the whole thing. I thought I had all my bases covered, but I forgot about her. I never even met her but when she got out, she was hooked up with a new Range Rover and a place to live for keeping her mouth shut. Plus a tidy, let's say, cash settlement. How's that for being ungrateful?"

"What do you mean you never met her?"

"When I was brought in to that hospital, I was unconscious. Got shot in the head in an assassination attempt."

"So, she helped save your life and you tried to kill her."

Mongo chuckles, "I guess she did. Ain't that a bitch. You sayin' she ain't dead yet. I ain't heard from my man since he had to shoot my idiot nephew's head off."

"You should give him a call?" I say, "I'm sure he'd love to talk to you."

"We have a strict no-call rule here, thanks. And he'll be back."

"Maybe," Elise says. "He's having a bit of a rough time, though. If he comes to, he might be pretty pissed at you, and you know what happens when people get pissed... they get a little mouthy."

"I'll cross that bridge when I come – Brandy, watch out!"

Brandy goes down quick, face-first into the marsh, and is pulled back by a very, very pissed-off alligator. She's screaming, but the screams don't last. The alligator's mouth clamps down on her side and rips half her torso off.

Mongo opens fire, emptying his clip into the beast. It falls dead next to its prey. Mongo is yelling and kicking the dead reptile, calling it every name in the book. He drops to his knees, quickly grabs the shotgun from the marsh, and swings it at my knee. I go down hard. I hear a shotgun blast but don't know where it was aimed. I yell for Elise while trying to get to my feet and cut around the other side of the shack.

"I'm okay!" Elise yells back. "I don't know where Mongo went! Be careful!"

I enter the shack by stepping on the generator and hoisting myself through the same window the stone-cold fox must have climbed out of to get the drop on us. I cut through the living room and out the front door just in time to see Mongo point the shotgun at Elise's back.

I dive towards her and hear the shots - lots of them. With Elise in my arms as we hit the ground, I realize it isn't gunfire at all. It's those goddamn fireworks.

Mongo turns frantically to see what's happening and is met with a metal detector smashed across his big dumb goddamn face, courtesy of my new best friend, Jamie.

"Hurry!" she yells, reaching down to help us up.

"Watch out!" Eric yells.

Mongo is down but not out. He's staggering on his feet like a stunned boxer, still managing to pump another round into the shotgun.

"I dropped my gun again!" Elise yells.

"There," Eric yells, pointing to the gun resting against the wall of the shack.

"Get back, Eric! Go!"

Elise and I both dive for the gun just as Mongo turns and fires off a round. The glass we were standing in front of mere seconds ago shatters.

Elise gets the gun and aims, but it doesn't matter. It's too late. The pissed-off alligator had a friend, and that son of a bitch just bit off Mongo's leg. No joke! I've never seen such a thing.

Mongo's yelling is causing even more unseen critters to flee into the darkness.

The alligator discards the leg and moves higher up, clenching his jaws down on Mongo's groin. The screams are deafening but fade as he is dragged below the water.

"Holy shit!" Eric yells from the trees.

"I told you to get back!" Elise yells.

"Leaving in the face of danger isn't something the Little Lemons Detective Agency does, Mom.

He steps from the tree, Elliot, and Milo behind him, each armed with fireworks and branches.

ELiSE

I want to throw up.

Like, for real, I want to throw up.

Instead, Jamie gives me her hand for the second time in as many minutes and pulls me to my feet. Archie next.

I'm in shock and completely silent. I have no idea what to say or do. It takes me what feels like thirty minutes to snap out of it, but when I do, I wrap my arms around my best friend so tightly she might not be able to breathe.

"All of you," I say. "I need all of you."

Everyone joins me in a big group hug, and my need to barf slowly vanishes like the screams of one Francis Giuseppe.

When the hug breaks, everyone just stands there in stunned silence. Apparently, I'm not the only one in shock. Archie is the first to move, so all eyes are on him when he whips out those stupid aviator glasses, snaps them open, puts them on dramatically, and says in his best David Carusso voice, "That's one alligator... I don't... want to see later."

Cue *The Who.*

Yeaaaahhhhhhhhhhh!

I don't know if the joke was the funniest thing we've all ever heard or if we were just desperate for some tension release, but we're all laughing so hard we're crying.

Unable to keep a straight face, Archie says, "Well, uh, ya know, we're still in an awful lot of danger out here. Remember when those two alligators killed those people... right here? Ha, yeah, so uh, maybe we should wrap this up and go back to the car."

In the distance, Gene and his merry band of men

have their sirens blaring. Not the best choice if we had been relying on a surprise attack.

"Boys," Archie says, "grab that leg over there. We'll probably need it."

Move to Florida, I said. It'll be great, I said.

Actually, it doesn't get much greater than this.

I want to tackle my kids and squeeze them so tight, but I know they won't let me.

Plus, Elliot is holding a man's severed leg right now.

I know who will let me hug on them, though.

Gary.

Let's go get Gary.

"This is the best Fourth of July everrrrr," Milo yells for the second time today as the squad cars all pull up.

"Literally ever," Elliot says, jumping up and down in the mud.

Eric high-fives his buddies. They're all smiles. They have no idea the real danger they were in. And it's my fault.

I can't think about that right now. We're all safe. We solved two cases in two hours and... wow... just wow. This family of mine, I swear.

They don't come much better than this.

I'm the luckiest woman alive.

ARCHiE

Despite it being super dark in the Wetlands, once we hit the main highway, the sun had just barely gone down, the sky still glowing from its presence.

Elise called Liz and Our Monica and told them we were on our way home, failing to leave out the part about Milo being out of the car in the swamp, but praising his metal detecting skills and successfully putting away a serial murderer.

It takes us less than thirty minutes to get home once we get out of the swamp, and our street is set up for a party. Tabitha and her daughters have lined up lawn chairs in front of our house and are sitting, waiting for the fireworks show to start. Down the street, Liz and Our Monica are walking towards us, Gary unsteadily leading the way.

We're quite the sight when we all get out of the car. Liz and Monica see their son and run to him. "What happened?"

"I fell in some mud. Don't worry. I caught a murderer."

I slowly back away, hoping they don't notice me. I've gotten in trouble with them before and would like to never have that happen again.

Eric and Elliot, the master bullshitters they are, run around to Milo and back up his story with such glee, his moms have no choice but to believe them. In fact, they don't even have time to be worried anymore because the boys are already in the street, filthy, setting up the fireworks. Brioni and her older sister Reese join in the fun.

"Well," I say to Elise, "I guess the party is starting."

"You smell like swamp trash," Elise says, wrapping her arms around my waist.

"You guys... okay?" Liz asks.

"Couldn't be better. Don't worry. Milo wasn't in any danger."

"We've learned to trust you, Archie. You're a pretty good guy. You might make some questionable decisions, but I know there is no way you would ever let something bad happen to our boy."

"Not a chance."

"Come on," Elise says to us, "the show is starting."

She takes my hand in hers, and we walk to the street where the kids are lighting off five fireworks simultaneously.

Behind us, over Cape Canaveral, the big ones start exploding in the sky.

Milo was right. This is the best Fourth of July ever. Even Gary is holding a sparkler.

What a day.

What a place.

What a life.

We sit on the curb, and Elise wraps her arm in mine and rests her head on my shoulder.

What a girl.

TWO
WEEKS
LATER

ARCHiE

The woman from the Cline Center came when she said she would and evaluated Gary. She confirmed what we already knew, and that's okay. The good news is, he'll be able to start a special school in September, the same time as the other kids. This will ensure he gets as much help as possible. It's not going to be easy for him, but he's sure got one hell of a support system.

As for Lowell Harmon, the sheriff's department did a thorough search of his house and came up with a handwritten hit list. As it turns out, by stopping him, we saved at least four more lives. Possibly double that if you include the randoms he was having killed to throw suspicion.

In hindsight, it wasn't that great of a plan, but as it turns out, Lowell really is dying. I think finding out who was blackmailing him before he died was the top priority, no matter the cost.

He'll die in prison.

As for Frank Giuseppe, AKA Mongo, we were spot on. The only thing we didn't figure was the brother's wife, but that didn't matter. He killed his brother and was going to swap places with him when the heat cooled.

His pyramid scheme, predictably, crumbled like it was bound to do sooner or later anyway.

Sarah Benson was glad to be rid of the money. It was weighing too much on her conscience even before she knew where it came from.

I paid her four times what it's worth, at Elise's insistence, but it doesn't matter - that truck is mine now. I dropped it off at a shop right after getting it to have a few leaks and the AC fixed and to get the awful stench of cigarettes out of there, but I can pick it up tomorrow. I can't wait.

The other hired terminal hitmen haven't been discovered yet. Honestly, who cares? They'll probably all be dead soon, if they're not already. There's no point in not letting the families keep the money. Or at least giving them the option to keep it.

I know that sounds awful, but who am I to judge someone else. It's none of my business so I will just butt out.

Nobody cares what I think anyway. That's a police matter, and my twenty-minute stint as a deputy of the Palm Beach Sherriff's Department has come to an end.

As for Elise's theater; it is coming along nicely. We went inside of it last week, and it's just... great. Nothing too fancy, but the stage is finished, along with most of the seating. The curtains and all the technical stuff is next. If everything goes according to schedule, it looks like she'll be able to open it in the fall. I'm hoping it's ready to go by Halloween, though. That could be a whole lot of fun.

I'm so proud of her.

Last night, Elise, Jamie, and I broke into the jerky frat-boys' apartment, slit the under-lining of both their mattresses, and stuffed in some dead fish we found along the coastline. I am perfectly aware of how childish and petty this is and I am totally fine with it.

Now, I know what you're thinking.

Monica.

Well...

I take a deep breath, grab the microphone and step on stage. I can hear my wife, kids, and friends cheering from the back row.

Someone out in the crowd just booed me, though.

Wiseguy.

"Hey everyone," I say to the crowd.

Another boo.

"Hey guys," I say to the band. "Before I get started, let me introduce the band. They don't get nearly as much credit as they deserve. *This* incredibly cool human is Ziggy."

Ziggy takes a bow.

"And *this* amazing human is Mitzi."

She curtsies.

"And behind me, on the drums... well, she's incredibly tough. Brave. And a hell of a fighter. This is Monica."

Monica, her head still wrapped in a bandage, waves to the crowd.

"These guys are the reason I'm up here because I sure as hell wouldn't be up here of my own free will. They promised my wife they would get me up here if we did them a small favor. Well, I guess we did the favor, and now I have to be up here. It's cool, though. I don't mind."

I take a deep breath and a moment for myself before I continue on.

"So, if you guys were here for 90's night a couple weeks ago, you might recognize my wife. She's the gorgeous brunette in the back." Much louder cheers than I got.

"And," I continue, "she will tell you that she's a die-hard pop-punk girl. If you ask her what her favorite album is, she might say 'Through Being Cool' by Saves the Day, or 'Dude Ranch.' She'd tell you her favorite songs were 'Sell My Old Clothes, I'm Off to Heaven,' or 'Carousel,' or 'Konstantine.'

"She'll wear the shirts and know all the words to every pop punk song there is... and all that is true. But what you don't know is that her all-time favorite song isn't pop-punk at all. I don't think anyone knows what her favorite song is... except me. And now the band. And soon to be you.

"We're going to play it for you here tonight, but with a little twist. Elise doesn't know this, but I've been working with the band for the past few days and we came up with a pop-punk version of the song. And it debuts tonight. We really hope you like it."

To Ziggy, I say, "So, you ready?"

"Oh, I'm ready," Ziggy says, smiling.

"Mitz?"

"Always."

"Mon?"

Monica hits her sticks together three times and the band comes alive with a tune instantly recognizable for any child of the 80s, only faster and without all that lame synth.

Also missing, one of the most iconic music videos ever made. But I'll try to make this work.

I take another deep breath and start singing.

"Talking away, I don't know what I'm to say."

The crowd cheers me on as I keep going. It's a song that is impossible to dislike.

"Shying away, I'll be comin' for your love, okay, take on me."

"Take on me!" the crowd roars.

"Take me on."

"Take me on!"

"I'll be gone in a day or two."

In the back, Elise is on her feet, jumping up and down, tears streaming down her face. Her face is pure happiness. Her smile ignites my soul.

"You're all the things I've got to remember."

When we finish the song, Monica walks around her drums and tackles me with a hug. I seem to be more worried about her head than she is. I feel Mitzi and Ziggy jump in, but more follow. After just a few seconds, it's a full on dog-pile. I can hear Elise and Jamie both laughing. They're piled up there somewhere.

I can't see who else is up there, but I have a sneaking suspicion.

It's the next afternoon and Elise and I are sitting in the back of my new piece of crap truck. We're backed up onto the beach, our legs stretched out on a blanket to protect us from the red hot metal. Our backs are resting against the back of the cab. Elise is in a bikini top and cut-off shorts, her head on my shoulder as we stare out at the ocean and a group of rowdy kids playing in it. The oldest, fixated with Jamie in a bikini, laying on her towel and getting a tan. The youngest, building a sandcastle with Milo, Brioni, and her family.

Gary is supervising the activities from his shaded beach chair.

Elise grabs my hand and intertwines her fingers in mine. "So this is why you wanted the truck?"

"It is."

"Well," she says, moving my hand to her lap, "I love it. And I love you." She kisses me on the lips then puts her head back on my shoulder as our kids and best friends laugh and play down below.

Florida, man.

Florida.

Visit the Archie and Elise Shop on Etsy for official Archie and Elise merch!

Etsy.com/Shop/ArchieAndElise

Follow Archie and Elise on Facebook.

Facebook.com/ArchieAndElise

Follow Grant on social media!

Instagram: GrantFieldgrove2.0
TikTok: GrantFieldgrove2.0
Facebook: Grant Fieldgrove

Thank you for reading this book!

If you're a long-time fan of Archie and Elise, or if this is your first introduction to them, I want to thank you from the bottom of my heart for checking them out.

Also, many thanks for Julie and McClane who had to deal with me being locked in my office while I wrote this.

I recently ventured into the business of movie making and have met some of the raddest people ever - so a big thanks to my *Time's Up* and *GSOB* buddies. I can't wait to work with you all again very soon.

Another big thanks to Lindsey for always grading my work, Jackson for being a constant supporter, Damian for trusting me with an epic amount of work and responsibility, and Monica for giving me some much needed nursing advice.

And last but not least, this book is fiction and I have nothing against Florida or its residents. It's a very fun place to visit. I promise.
It is, also, a comedy and not a hard-boiled police procedural. Thanks for not judging it based on its realism, or lack thereof.
Any Florida resident or anyone familiar with a map, for that matter, will realize I took several liberties with locations. That's the beauty of writing fiction – I can just make up stuff whenever I want. Sunrise Cove does not exist, but Cocoa Beach, Cape Canaveral, and Palm Beach do. I've been to all three and my love for them and their warm beach water is what inspired my fictional town.
I look forward to revisiting it for several books to come.